LIVING WITH DISEASES AND DISORDERS

Cancer and Sickle Cell Disease

LIVING WITH DISEASES AND DISORDERS

ADHD and Other Behavior Disorders

Allergies and Other Immune System Disorders

Asthma, Cystic Fibrosis, and Other Respiratory Disorders

Autism and Other Developmental Disorders

Cancer and Sickle Cell Disease

Cerebral Palsy and Other Traumatic Brain Injuries

Crohn's Disease and Other Digestive Disorders

Depression, Anxiety, and Bipolar Disorders

Diabetes and Other Endocrine Disorders

Migraines and Seizures

Muscular Dystrophy and Other Neuromuscular Disorders

LIVING WITH DISEASES AND DISORDERS

Cancer and Sickle Cell Disease

H.W. POOLE

SERIES ADVISOR
HEATHER L. PELLETIER, Ph.D.
Pediatric Psychologist, Hasbro Children's Hospital
Clinical Assistant Professor, Warren Alpert Medical School of Brown University

MASON CREST

Mason Crest
450 Parkway Drive, Suite D
Broomall, PA 19008
www.masoncrest.com

© 2018 by Mason Crest, an imprint of National Highlights, Inc. All rights reserved. No part of this publication may be reproduced or transmitted in any form or by any means, electronic or mechanical, including photocopying, recording, taping, or any information storage and retrieval system, without permission from the publisher.

MTM Publishing, Inc.
435 West 23rd Street, #8C
New York, NY 10011
www.mtmpublishing.com

President: Valerie Tomaselli
Vice President, Book Development: Hilary Poole
Designer: Annemarie Redmond
Copyeditor: Peter Jaskowiak
Editorial Assistant: Leigh Eron

Series ISBN: 978-1-4222-3747-2
Hardback ISBN: 978-1-4222-3752-6
E-Book ISBN: 978-1-4222-8033-1

Library of Congress Cataloging-in-Publication Data
Names: Poole, Hilary W., author.
Title: Cancer and sickle cell disease / H.W. Poole.
Description: Broomall, PA: Mason Crest, [2018] | Series: Living with diseases and disorders | Audience: Age 12+ | Audience: Grade 7 to 8. | Includes index.
Identifiers: LCCN 2017007141 2018 (print) | LCCN 2017011787 (ebook) | ISBN 9781422280331 (ebook) | ISBN 9781422237526 (hardback : alk. paper)
Subjects: LCSH: Cancer in children—Juvenile literature. | Sickle cell anemia in children—Juvenile literature.
Classification: LCC RC281.C4 (ebook) | LCC RC281.C4 P62 2018 (print) | DDC 618.92/994—dc23
LC record available at https://lccn.loc.gov/2017007141

Printed and bound in the United States of America.

First printing
9 8 7 6 5 4 3 2 1

QR CODES AND LINKS TO THIRD PARTY CONTENT
You may gain access to certain third party content ("Third Party Sites") by scanning and using the QR Codes that appear in this publication (the "QR Codes"). We do not operate or control in any respect any information, products or services on such Third Party Sites linked to by us via the QR Codes included in this publication and we assume no responsibility for any materials you may access using the QR Codes. Your use of the QR Codes may be subject to terms, limitations, or restrictions set forth in the applicable terms of use or otherwise established by the owners of the Third Party Sites. Our linking to such Third Party Sites via the QR Codes does not imply an endorsement or sponsorship of such Third Party Sites, or the information, products or services offered on or through the Third Party Sites, nor does it imply an endorsement or sponsorship of this publication by the owners of such Third Party Sites.

TABLE OF CONTENTS

Series Introduction 6
Chapter One: The C Word 9
Chapter Two: Kids and Cancer 21
Chapter Three: Living with Cancer 33
Chapter Four: Living with Sickle Cell Disease 47
Further Reading 57
Series Glossary 58
Index 60
About the Advisor 64
About the Author 64
Photo Credits 64

Key Icons to Look for:

Words to Understand: These words with their easy-to-understand definitions will increase the reader's understanding of the text, while building vocabulary skills.

Sidebars: This boxed material within the main text allows readers to build knowledge, gain insights, explore possibilities, and broaden their perspectives by weaving together additional information to provide realistic and holistic perspectives.

Educational Videos: Readers can view videos by scanning our QR codes, which will provide them with additional educational content to supplement the text. Examples include news coverage, moments in history, speeches, iconic sports moments, and much more.

Text-Dependent Questions: These questions send the reader back to the text for more careful attention to the evidence presented there.

Research Projects: Readers are pointed toward areas of further inquiry connected to each chapter. Suggestions are provided for projects that encourage deeper research and analysis.

Series Glossary of Key Terms: This back-of-the-book glossary contains terminology used throughout the series. Words found here increase the reader's ability to read and comprehend higher-level books and articles in this field.

SERIES INTRODUCTION

According to the Chronic Disease Center at the Centers for Disease Control and Prevention, over 100 million Americans suffer from a chronic illness or medical condition. In other words, they have a health problem that lasts three months or more, affects their ability to perform normal activities, and requires frequent medical care and/or hospitalizations. Epidemiological studies suggest that between 15 and 18 million of those with chronic illness or medical conditions are children and adolescents. That's roughly one out of every four children in the United States.

These young people must exert more time and energy to complete the tasks their peers do with minimal thought. For example, kids with Crohn's disease, ulcerative colitis, or other digestive issues have to plan meals and snacks carefully, to make sure they are not eating food that could irritate their stomachs or cause pain and discomfort. People with cerebral palsy, muscular dystrophy, or other physical limitations associated with a medical condition may need help getting dressed, using the bathroom, or joining an activity in gym class. Those with cystic fibrosis, asthma, or epilepsy may have to avoid certain activities or environments altogether. ADHD and other behavior disorders require the individual to work harder to sustain the level of attention and focus necessary to keep up in school.

Living with a chronic illness or medical condition is not easy. Identifying a diagnosis and adjusting to the initial shock is only the beginning of a long journey. Medications, follow-up appointments and procedures, missed school or work, adjusting to treatment regimens, coping with uncertainty, and readjusting expectations are all hurdles one has to overcome in learning how to live one's best life. Naturally, feelings of sadness or anxiety may set in while learning how to make it all work. This is especially true for young people, who may reach a point in their medical journey when they have to rethink some of their original goals and life plans to better match their health reality.

Chances are, you know people who live this reality on a regular basis. It is important to remember that those affected by chronic illness are family members, neighbors, friends, or maybe even our own doctors. They are likely navigating the demands of the day a little differently, as they balance the specific accommodations necessary to manage their illness. But they have the same desire to be productive and included as those who are fortunate not to have a chronic illness.

This set provides valuable information about the most common childhood chronic illnesses, in language that is engaging and easy for students to grasp. Each chapter highlights important vocabulary words and offers text-dependent questions to help assess comprehension. Meanwhile, educational videos (available by scanning QR codes) and research projects help connect the text to the outside world.

Our mission with this set is twofold. First, the volumes provide a go-to source for information about chronic illness for young people who are living with particular conditions. Each volume in this set strives to provide reliable medical information and practical advice for living day-to-day with various challenges. Second, we hope these volumes will also help kids without chronic illness better understand and appreciate how people with health challenges live. After all, if one in four young people is managing a health condition, it's safe to assume that the majority of our youth already know someone with a chronic illness, whether they realize it or not.

With the growing presence of social media, bullying is easier than ever before. It's vital that young people take a moment to stop and think about how they are more similar to kids with health challenges than they are different. Poor understanding and low tolerance for individual differences are often the platforms for bullying and noninclusive behavior, both in person and online. Living with Diseases and Disorders strives to close the gap of misunderstanding.

The ultimate solution to the bullying problem is surely an increase in empathy. We hope these books will help readers better understand and appreciate not only the daily struggles of people living with chronic conditions, but their triumphs as well.

—Heather Pelletier, Ph.D.
Hasbro Children's Hospital
Warren Alpert Medical School of Brown University

WORDS TO UNDERSTAND

benign: not harmful.

carcinogens: substances that can cause cancer to develop.

epithelial: a type of human tissue; includes the outer layer of skin and the lining of organs.

genes: units of hereditary information.

lymphatic system: part of the human immune system; transports white blood cells around the body.

malignant: harmful; relating to tumors, likely to spread.

mutation: a change in structure, particularly of a cell in this context.

prognosis: the likely outcome of a disease.

CHAPTER ONE

The C Word

Not so long ago, cancer was such a terrifying condition that it wasn't even discussed openly. It was essentially the Voldemort of diseases. In fact, it was often called "the C word," because people didn't even want to say the name out loud. Things have changed a lot since then, however. Today, people talk openly about cancer, and there are frequent public relations campaigns to spread the word about treatments and screening. Better still, people are beating cancer at higher rates than ever before.

It's important to understand that there are many different types of cancer, and a person's **prognosis** will vary on the type of cancer and the timing of the diagnosis. But in general, cancer is no longer the death sentence it was thought to be in the past. Since the 1970s, there has been a decrease in the number of new cases of most types of cancer, as well as an increase in the number of people who survive a cancer diagnosis.

Cell Division

Every person is composed of about 37 trillion cells, which come in more than 200 different types. These cells all have life spans, just like we ourselves do. We only

CANCER AND SICKLE CELL DISEASE

celebrate our birthdays once a year, but on a cellular level, we are being born constantly.

Some types of cells reproduce primarily when we're young—bone cells, for instance, do a lot of reproducing when we're growing, but they slow down once we've reached our full height. On the other hand, blood cells are being reproduced all the time. Blood cells are made inside our bones, by what's called bone marrow. The bone marrow of a healthy person creates about 7 million new blood cells every month.

In a process called *mitosis*, a cell reproduces by dividing into two identical copies of itself. Human cells can divide around 50 to 60 times (the exact number

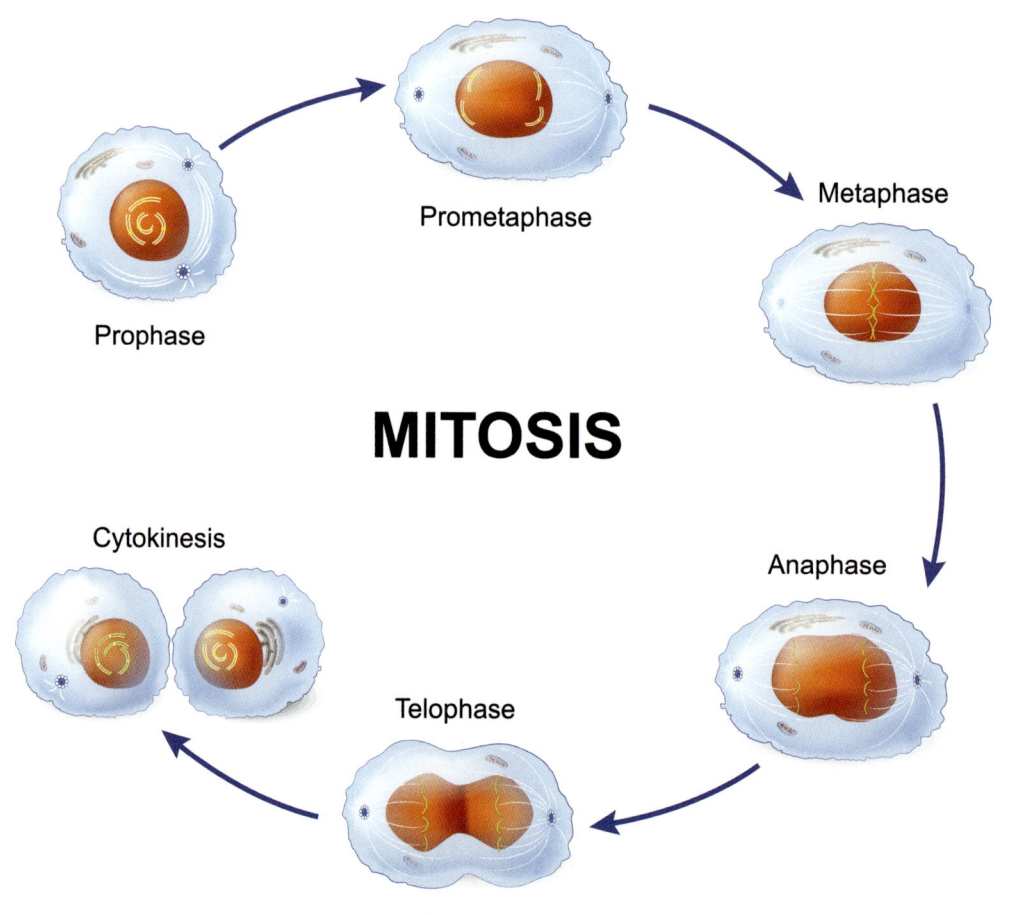

MITOSIS

The stages of cell reproduction, or mitosis.

depends on the type of cell); eventually they die and are replaced with new cells. Cell division is controlled by the DNA, or **genes**, that exist in each cell. In a healthy person, cell division is a controlled process that only happens when needed. For instance, if you cut your finger, the normal level of cell division in your skin will increase for a time, creating more skin cells to replace the damaged ones. Each new cell will be identical to the previous one, and the process will continue until the injury is healed. At that point, skin-cell division will return to its usual pace.

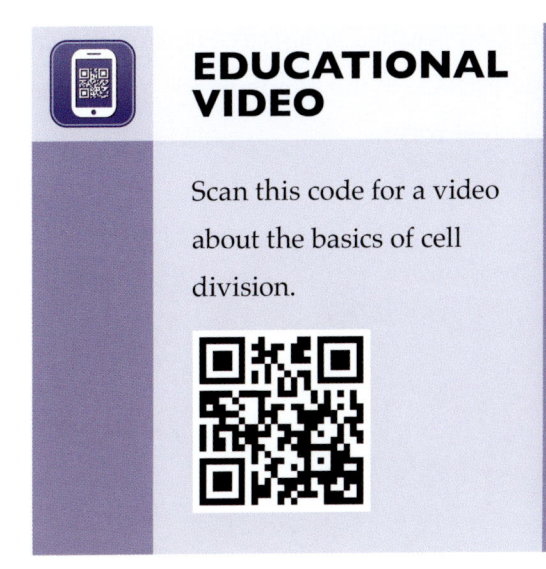

EDUCATIONAL VIDEO

Scan this code for a video about the basics of cell division.

But sometimes cell division goes wrong, and the new cell is *not* identical to the original. This is called a **mutation**. Mutations can happen randomly during cell division, when the DNA doesn't copy correctly, or they can be caused by external factors (more on this in the next section). Cell mutations are actually quite common, and they don't necessarily cause problems. Much of the time, mutated cells simply don't survive—the immune system wipes them out, or they die on their own. But sometimes that doesn't occur, and the mutated cells are able to reproduce themselves. These are called precancerous cells. Although they continue to fulfill their usual role, they can become a problem if they continue to mutate.

Out-of-control cell growth is a bit like the proverbial snowball rolling downhill: the more mutated cells there are, the more mutations will occur, and the harder it becomes for the body to stop the reproduction from happening. This is how cancer begins. Mutated cancer cells reproduce unchecked, and they often destroy nearby healthy cells, too. In time, cancer cells may travel throughout the body, usually through the **lymphatic system**, and invade other tissues. This

CANCER AND SICKLE CELL DISEASE

process is called *metastasis*. For example, cancer might start in the lungs, but then metastasize to the lymph nodes, and from there, it may travel to the bones, brain, or other organs.

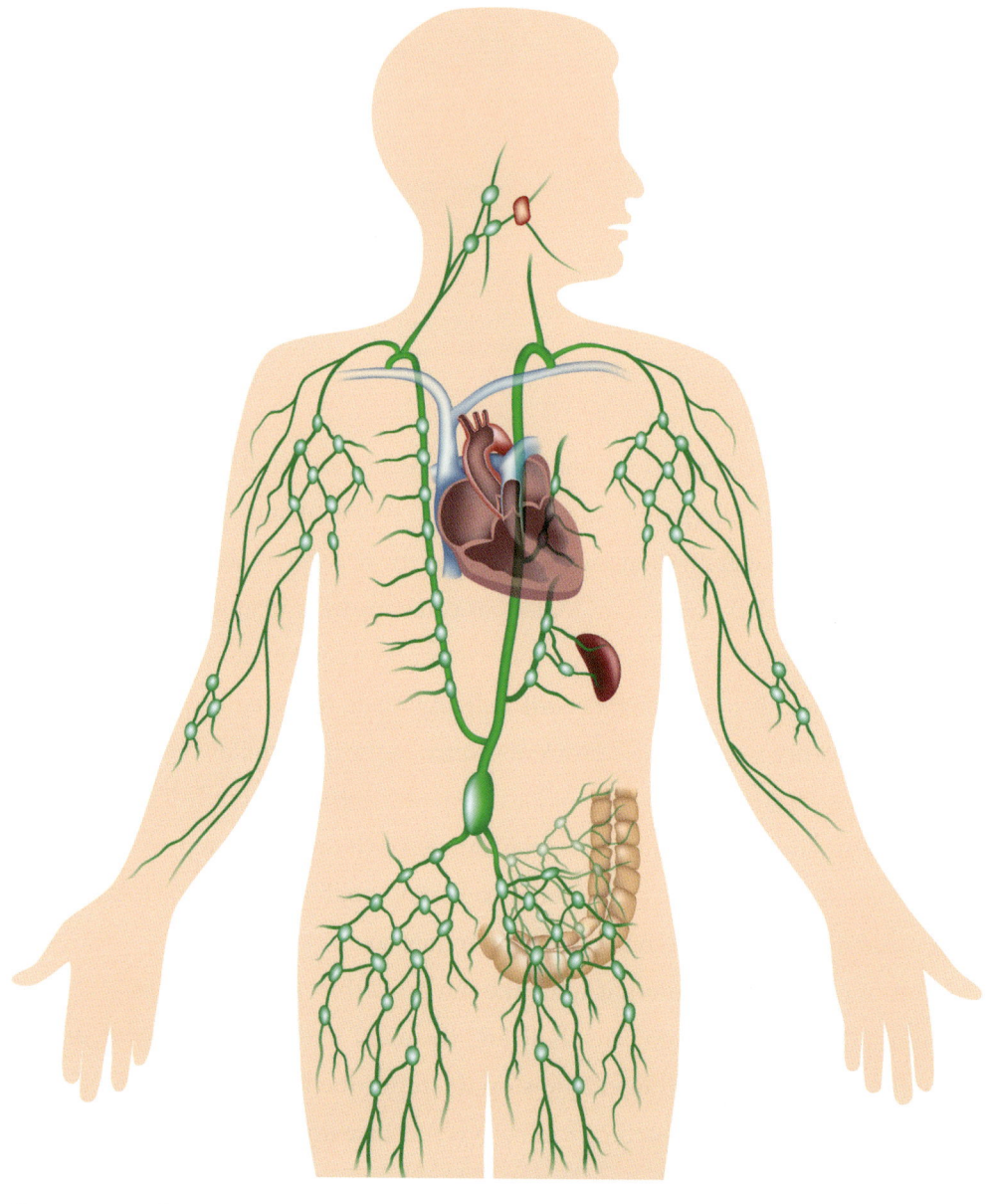

Cancerous cells use the lymphatic system to travel around the body.

THE C WORD

Causes of Cancer

In a basic sense, all types of cancer have the same cause. It all goes back to the cells that began replicating out of control. The real question is, what caused those mutations to occur in the first place? Unfortunately, the answers to that question are varied and complex, and in many cases they remain a mystery.

Because cancer involves genes, which are passed along from parents to their children, we do know that heredity plays a role. According to the National Cancer Institute, somewhere between 5 and 10 percent of all cancer cases are what are called *hereditary cancer syndromes*. In these cases, the people involved were born with particular genetic changes that led to their cancers. These mainly involve malignant tumors—breast cancer is probably the most famous type of cancer that tends to "run in families." But if you think about it, 5 to 10 percent

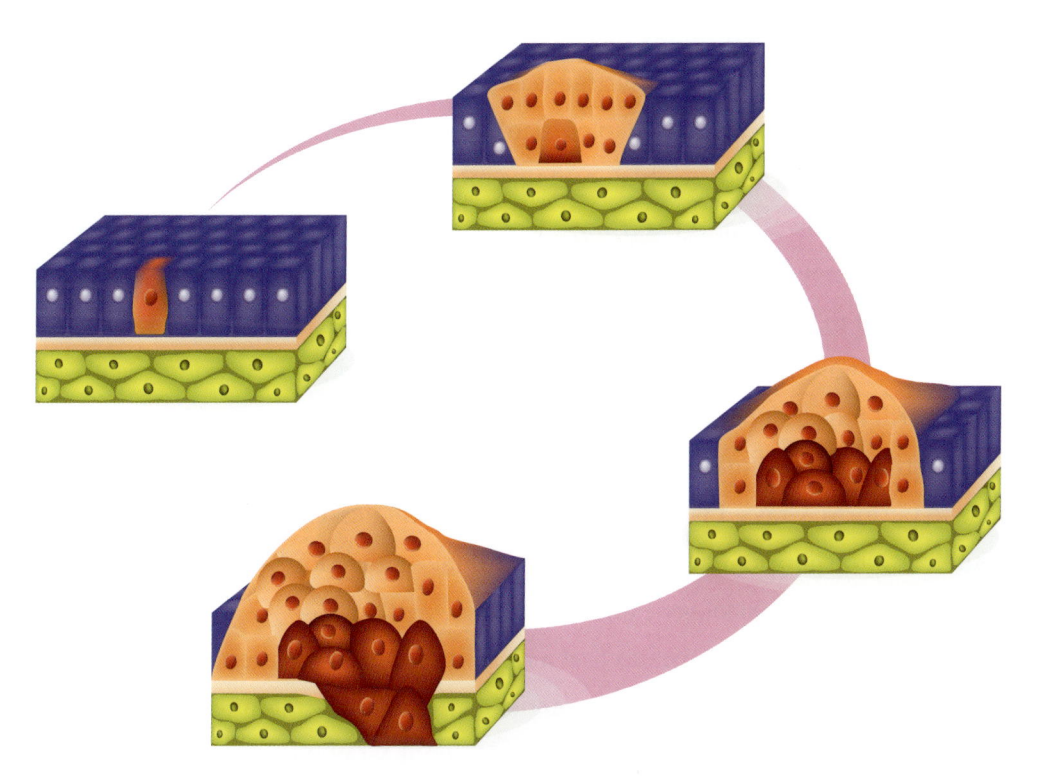

This diagram shows how cancer can begin with one cell and gradually progress.

13

of cases is actually not very many. That means that around 90 percent of cancer cases are *not* inherited directly. So where do those come from?

Although the vast majority cancers are not inherited in a direct way, you *can* inherit a greater risk for certain cancers. This is one reason doctors ask about your family medical history. Let's say that your father had colon cancer. The colon is part of the digestive system, and it can develop malignant tumors that are hard to treat. We know that the risk for colon cancer can be inherited, so your doctor might recommend that you be checked for colon cancer sooner or more often than a person whose parents never had the disease. Inheriting a risk does not mean that you will definitely develop cancer, however. It just means that your chances may be higher. Family history is just one part of the picture.

Genetic mutations that occur after a baby is conceived—meaning they did not come from the parents' DNA but developed on their own—are called *somatic* changes, which simply means they were acquired. We all have somatic mutations, and they don't always cause cancer. But the ones that do are sometimes caused by exposure to particular toxins, or **carcinogens**. The classic example is tobacco smoke, which contains many chemicals that are either suspected or proven cancer-causing agents. That's why cigarette smoking can cause cancer not only in the person who smokes, but also in other people who are exposed to the smoke.

Other known carcinogens include lead, which used to be added to gasoline and is still found in old paint; a material called asbestos, which used to be used in construction; and many forms of radiation, such as the machines that doctors use to perform X-rays. Lists of known and suspected carcinogens are kept by public health agencies such as the International Agency for Research on Cancer and the National Toxicology Program.

It's important to understand that a single exposure to a carcinogen is unlikely to cause cancer. Somatic mutations are not that straightforward. For instance, it's considered safe to have an occasional X-ray, as long as the radiation levels are low and you don't do it all the time. That's why the technician who

THE MUTANTS

Researchers have come a long way in figuring out precisely which genes are likely to cause problems. Two main types of genes are responsible for cancer: *oncogenes* and *tumor suppressor genes*. Both types help control when new cells are created, how quickly they grow, and when they die. Mutations in either type can result in the excessive cell division that is cancer.

For example, a gene called TP53 is a tumor suppressor: it creates a protein that limits the growth of tumors. Mutations in the TP53 gene are one of the most common factors found in people with hereditary cancer syndrome. Meanwhile, a mutated oncogene called HER2 has been found in about 30 percent of breast cancers.

does the X-ray will step behind a protective shield—she *is* around X-rays all the time, so she does have to be careful about her exposure levels.

When it comes to cancer, researchers suspect that it's actually a complex blend of genes and environment that causes the problem. For example, let's imagine a particular family, who by virtue of being related have certain genetic similarities. In this family, Mom smokes, Dad smokes, and Grandad smokes. Over time, a number of people in the family develop lung cancer. Was it environment or heredity? The answer is probably, some of both.

Types of Cancer

One challenging aspect of cancer is just how many types there are. Not only that, but each person's cancer can be quite different from anyone else's. This has big implications for treatment, as we'll see later.

CANCER AND SICKLE CELL DISEASE

CANCER LOCATIONS

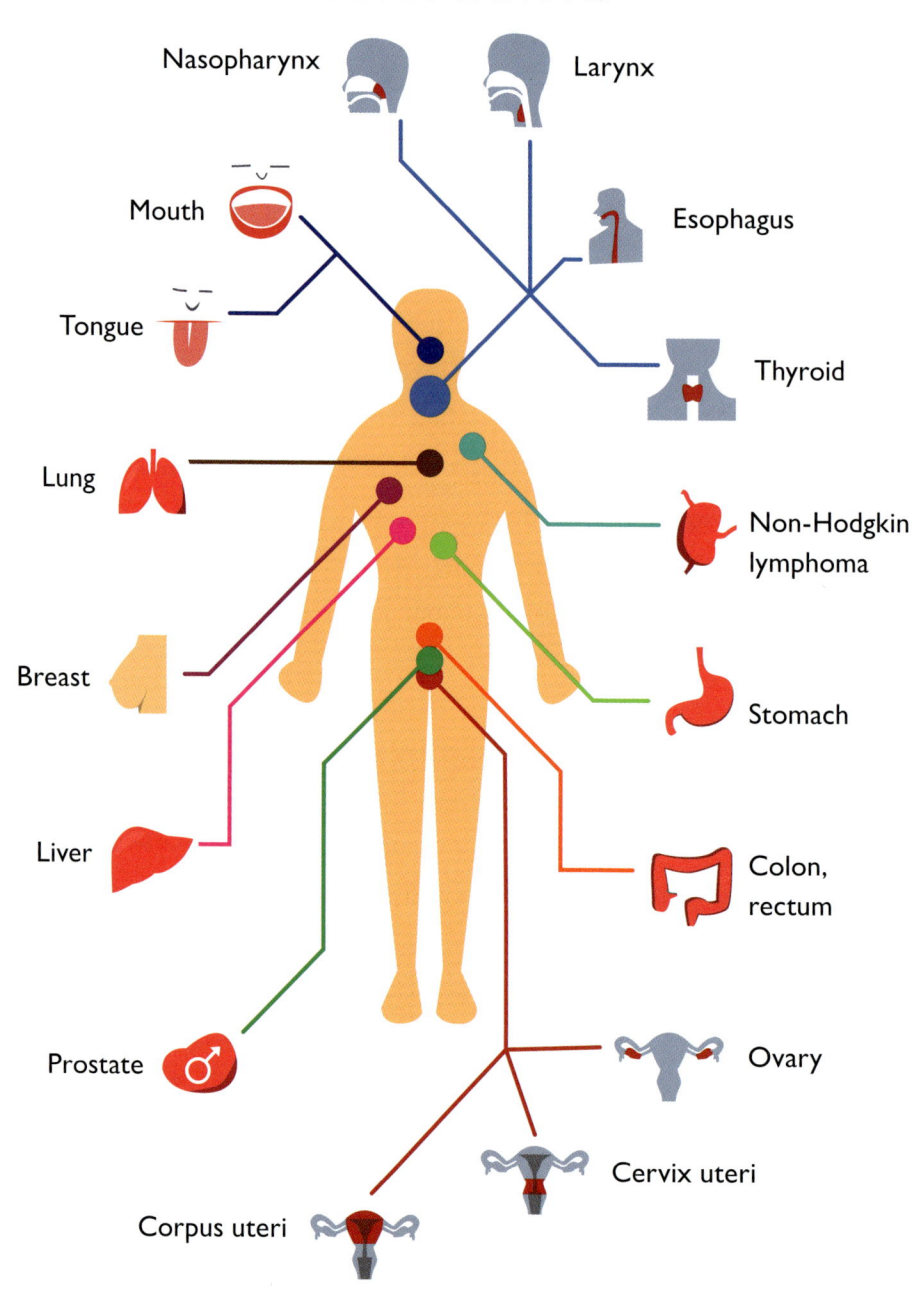

Nasopharynx
Larynx
Mouth
Esophagus
Tongue
Thyroid
Lung
Non-Hodgkin lymphoma
Breast
Stomach
Liver
Colon, rectum
Prostate
Ovary
Cervix uteri
Corpus uteri

Cancer can develop in any part of the body; this diagram shows some of the most common areas.

THE C WORD

There are six general types of cancer: carcinoma, sarcoma, melanomas, lymphoma, leukemia, and central nervous system tumors. The rest of this chapter provides a brief overview of each type. More detailed information about certain cancers affecting kids can be found in chapter two.

Carcinomas are cancers that grow in what are called **epithelial** cells, including skin tissue, the lining of internal organs, and the lining of body cavities. Lung, bladder, and stomach cancers are all carcinomas. Carcinomas are much more common in adults than in young people. Many of them seem to be caused by exposure to particular toxins, cigarette smoke being the most obvious example. The most common skin cancers are also carcinomas. Fortunately, skin carcinomas are also one of the most treatable types of cancer—they can be completely cured about 95 percent of the time.

Sarcomas are cancers that grow in bones and in the body's connective tissue—tendons, cartilage, and so on. Sarcomas are not very common at all. But when they do occur, they often happen to young people. The Sarcoma Alliance reports that of all adults with cancer, only 1 percent have a sarcoma. But among all young people with cancer, 15 percent have a sarcoma.

Melanomas are another type of skin cancer. They appear as dark areas on the surface of the skin. If you hear someone talking about "getting a mole checked," that person is referring to a possible melanoma. Unlike skin carcinomas, which usually don't spread, melanomas can be aggressive. Melanomas need to be treated right away, so that the cancer cells can't spread to the rest of the body. Kids can develop melanomas, but it's quite rare for that to happen. According to the Dana Farber Cancer Institute, only around 200 young people develop a melanoma in the United States every year.

Lymphoma is a type of cancer that begins in the white blood cells (or *lymphocytes*) of the immune system. There are two types of lymphoma, Hodgkin and non-Hodgkin; the latter is far more common, with 70,000 new cases a year, as opposed to only 8,000 new cases of Hodgkin lymphoma. Non-Hodgkin lymphoma can occur at any age, but it tends to occur in older people—the average age of a

CANCER AND SICKLE CELL DISEASE

SMOKING AND CANCER

Despite decades of industry denial, it's now well established that cigarettes and cancer are directly linked. The connection between smoking and numerous types of cancer is clear and has been established repeatedly, not only in medical studies but also in the courts. In 2016, for example, the widow of a man who died of lung cancer was awarded $23.6 billion in her lawsuit against the R.J. Reynolds Tobacco Company.

Unfortunately, the causes of many other cancers are not nearly as clear-cut. But if you want to avoid cancer, the single most important thing to do is not smoke. Smoking doesn't just cause lung and throat cancer; it has also been connected to cancers in the liver, the bladder, the stomach, the colon, and more.

non-Hodgkin lymphoma patient is around 60. Hodgkin lymphoma, on the other hand, strikes people who are either in their late teens or their early 60s.

Leukemia is another type of cancer involving blood cells. But leukemias (plural because there are actually a number of different types) originate in the bone marrow, which is where blood is made. The bone marrow of someone with leukemia creates mutated white blood cells that don't function the way they're supposed to.

The final category of cancers is *central nervous system* (*CNS*) *tumors*, such as brain tumors and tumors of the spinal cord. Not all CNS tumors are cancer; many are **benign**, meaning they don't spread. They do grow, however, which can be a big problem in and of itself. **Malignant** tumors both grow and spread beyond the CNS.

Who Is to Blame?

The media frequently reports that a certain product may cause cancer, while a certain other product might prevent it. For example, many consumers seek out food containing antioxidants like vitamin C and vitamin E, which are believed to be cancer fighters. We are instructed to not just avoid tobacco, but also to exercise more, eat less red meat, and so on, all in the hopes of warding off the "C word."

This is all good advice, and the benefits of a healthy lifestyle stretch far beyond the cancer question. But there is a dark side to all this cheerleading: people with cancer are sometimes made to feel like it's their fault. A cancer diagnosis starts to sound like some sort of judgment. After all, there are mountains of books and articles about how to avoid cancer—so if you get it anyway, you must have done something wrong.

This is not true. Yes, avoiding known carcinogens is a good choice whenever possible. But we often don't know why some cells mutate, just as we don't know why some mutations become malignant. Genetic mutations don't care whether we make "good" choices or "bad" ones. Cancer is a disease, not a moral judgment on the people who have it.

Text-Dependent Questions

1. Roughly what percentage of cancer cases are directly inherited?
2. What are some examples of carcinogens?
3. What are the six major types of cancer?

Research Project

Research common carcinogens, like the ones mentioned in this chapter. Find out how and when their cancer-causing nature was discovered. What happened next? Write a brief report about your findings.

WORDS TO UNDERSTAND

anemia: an illness caused by a lack of red blood cells.
localized: limited to a small area.
myeloid: relating to bone marrow.
recurrence: when something happens again.
undifferentiated: two or more things that are completely alike and can't be told apart.

CHAPTER TWO

Kids and Cancer

As discussed in chapter one, some types of cancer are more common in young people than others. This book is too short to cover every single type, but this chapter will focus on the most common ones: leukemia, lymphoma, and childhood sarcomas.

In Your Bones

We've all seen models of human skeletons—in doctors' offices, in museums, even in stores that sell Halloween decorations. But these models can trick you into thinking that human bones are just solid chunks of calcium, with not much going on. In fact, nothing could be further from the truth. Your bones are much more than just a framework for your organs and skin. Your bones are alive.

Bones have three basic components: compact bone, spongy bone, and bone marrow. The compact bone is the hard shell that runs along the outside, the spongy bone is at the ends, and the bone marrow is in the center. Bone marrow comes in two basic types: yellow marrow, which is mostly fat, and red marrow, which creates new blood cells. Different bones have different amounts of each

CANCER AND SICKLE CELL DISEASE

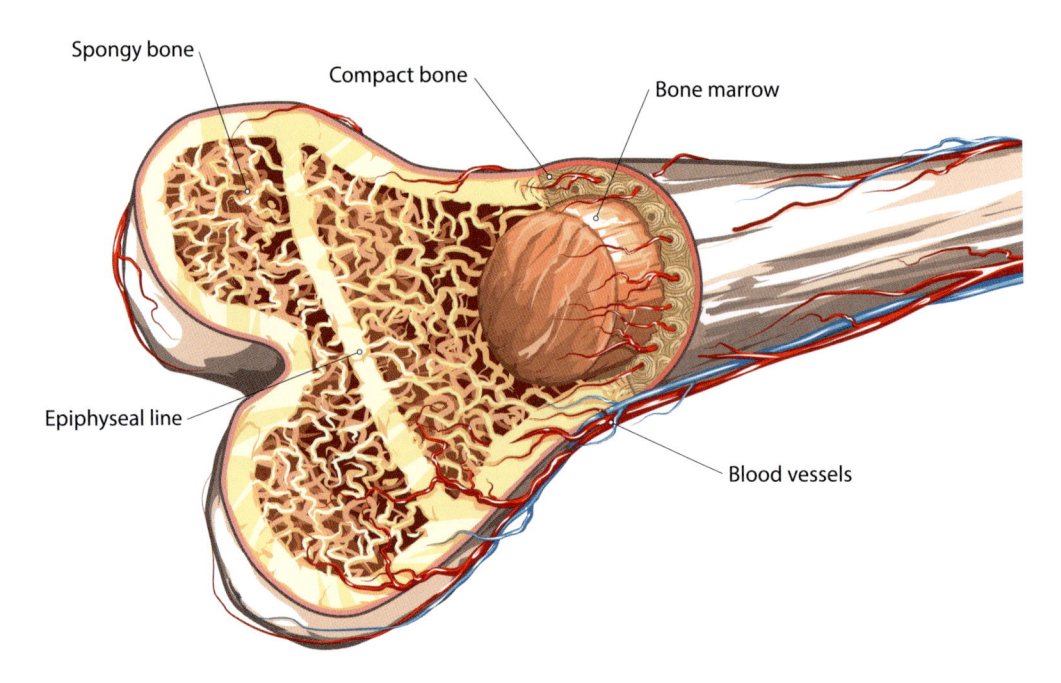

The major parts of a human bone.

type of marrow. You also have different amounts of bone marrow at various points in your life—infants have tons of red marrow, but as people age, their yellow marrow gradually increases and red marrow decreases.

Red marrow creates stem cells, which are large, **undifferentiated** cells that can develop into a variety of more specialized cells. Stem cells are sometimes called "immature" cells. They can respond to particular conditions in the body, making more of one type of cell when it's needed, and then switching over to making a different type when that's needed. Stem cells create a variety of specialized cells, such as red blood cells (also called *erythrocytes*) and white blood cells (also called *lymphocytes*), and others.

There are two main types of cancer that can result from problems with blood marrow: leukemia and lymphoma. (Sickle cell disease is *not* a form of cancer, but it does also relate to blood and bone marrow; it's discussed in chapter four.)

Leukemia

Leukemias are the most common type of childhood cancer, with around 5,000 new cases diagnosed annually. According to the American Cancer Society, nearly one in every three cases of childhood cancer is a form of leukemia.

The most common type (about 75 percent) is called childhood acute lymphoblastic leukemia (ALL). ALL gets its name from the fact that it develops in lymphocytes. It most commonly occurs between the ages of two and four. A second type of childhood leukemia, acute myeloid leukemia (AML), also starts in the white blood cells, but it happens to **myeloid** cells, not lymphocytes. AML can happen any time during childhood, but it tends to occur either before the age of two or in teenagers. The survival rate for AML is very high—nearly 93 percent. ALL, on the other hand, is a more aggressive form of leukemia. Still, more than 65 percent of kids who are diagnosed will survive five years or more.

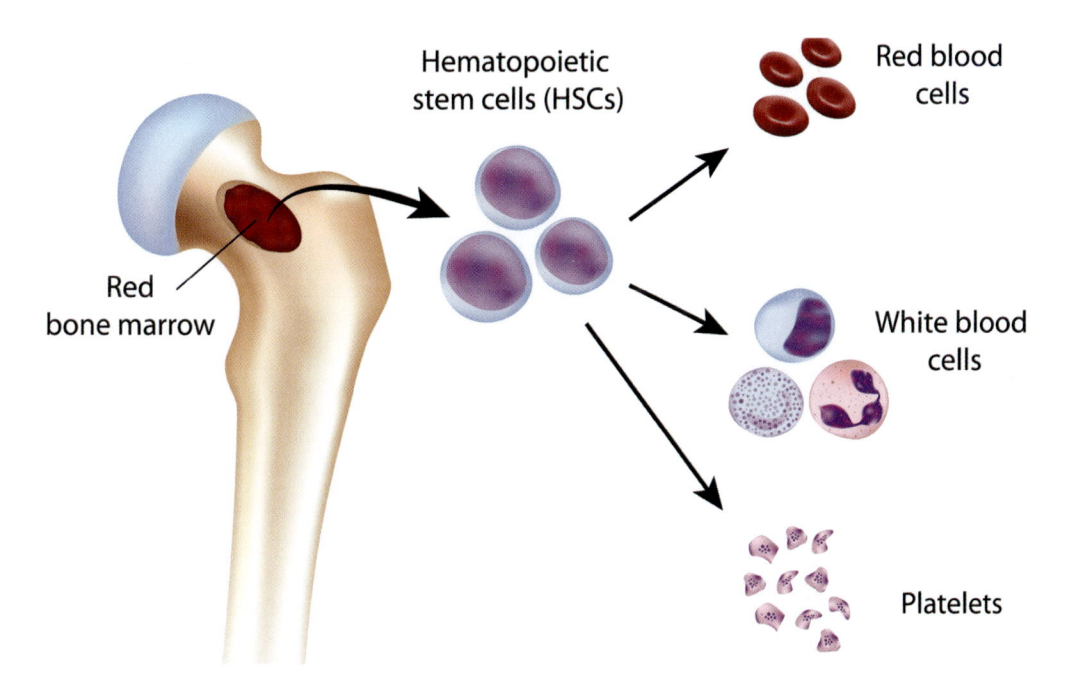

Stem cells in bone marrow can grow into three main types of specialized cells.

CANCER AND SICKLE CELL DISEASE

Both ALL and AML result in an overproduction of malfunctioning white blood cells. This results in two main health problems. First, the immune systems of people with leukemia are severely compromised because their white blood cells are malfunctioning. Second, the malignant cells continue to grow and take up space in the bone marrow, which makes it more difficult for the marrow to do its job well.

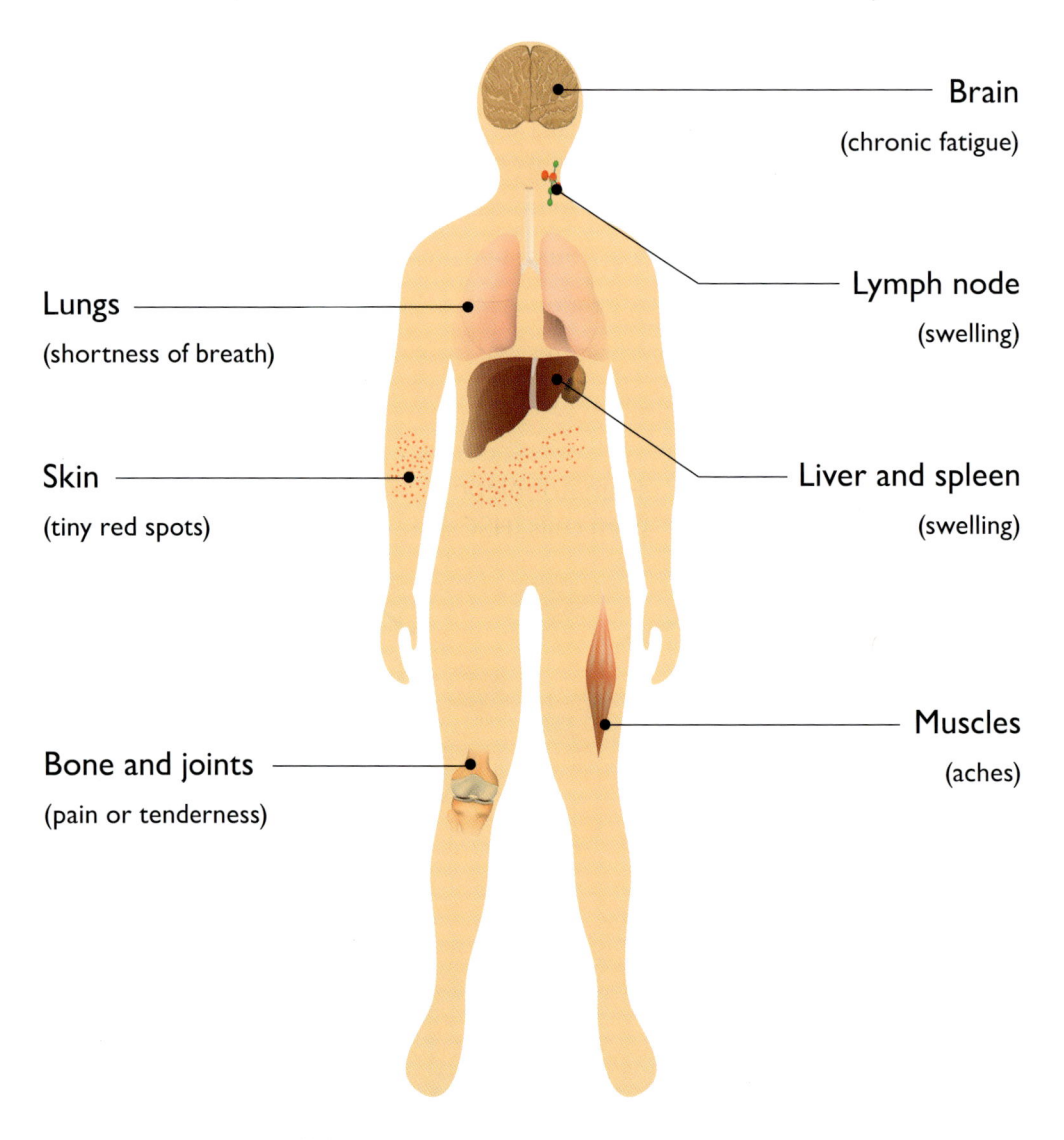

Brain (chronic fatigue)

Lymph node (swelling)

Lungs (shortness of breath)

Liver and spleen (swelling)

Skin (tiny red spots)

Muscles (aches)

Bone and joints (pain or tenderness)

The major symptoms of leukemia.

UNDERSTANDING SURVIVAL RATES

When we get sick and go to the doctor, we want to hear, "Take this pill and your illness will go away for good." And that certainly can happen. For instance, antibiotics do a tremendous job at curing some illnesses.

On the other end of the spectrum are illnesses that can't be cured, but can only be managed. We call these chronic illnesses—things like type 1 diabetes, Crohn's disease, epilepsy, and sickle cell disease (discussed later in this book). While doctors can't make these conditions disappear, modern medicine can help people live with them.

Most cancers are slightly different from either of those situations. Let's say someone has a tumor, and the tumor is removed through surgery. Another person has ALL and successfully completes chemotherapy. It would be nice to say that both of these people are "cured." Unfortunately, cancer cells can come back at any point; doctors call this a **recurrence**.

Because "cure" is a misleading word when it comes to cancer, doctors prefer to talk about a "survival rate." Patients who are still alive five years after their cancer diagnosis are considered *essentially* cured, but not totally. Most people who have survived cancer will continue to be monitored for recurrence for years.

Because of the damage that leukemias do to the immune system, the initial symptoms often look very much like typical colds or flu: fever, general fatigue, sore joints, and infections such as bronchitis. The condition called **anemia** is also very common. People with leukemia also tend to bruise or bleed easily, because malfunctioning bone marrow makes it harder for the body to heal itself. Sometimes they have stomach pain, which is caused by all the malformed cells building up in the liver and kidneys. Leukemias are diagnosed through blood tests and by removing a tiny amount of bone marrow so that it can be studied under a microscope.

Leukemias are usually treated with chemotherapy, in which cancer-killing drugs are administered either intravenously or in pill form. Depending on the situation, some kids with leukemia may use other treatments as well. Most importantly, stem cell transplants replace malfunctioning cells with healthy ones. Sometimes this can be done with the patients' own cells, but other times a donor is needed. The process used to be called "bone marrow transplant," because it involved replacing the red bone marrow entirely. These days, doctors are able to just focus on replacing the stem cells themselves.

Lymphoma

White blood cells, which are the body's primary disease fighters, are transported around the body in a liquid called *lymph*. The lymph is filtered at spots around the body called *nodes*—you have lymph nodes in your neck, under your arms, and in your groin, among other places. That's why your throat gets swollen when you're sick—the lymphatic system is working overtime to kill whatever virus or bacteria is making you ill.

However, genetic mutations in lymphocytes can result in an overproduction of cells. As mentioned in chapter one, there are two main types of lymphoma: Hodgkin and non-Hodgkin. It's possible for kids to develop either type, but Hodgkin lymphoma is far more likely to happen to people in their late teens and early 20s, and so it will be our focus here.

Hodgkin lymphomas (sometimes called Hodgkin's disease) is named in honor of the British physician Sir Thomas Hodgkin. Hodgkin was a pioneer in many ways—he was apparently the first to use a stethoscope at his hospital, for example. He first wrote about a condition involving abnormal lymph nodes in 1832, and his name was given to the disease by another doctor in 1865.

Like leukemia, initial symptoms of lymphoma can look a bit like the flu—including fever, weakness, and fatigue. Sore, swollen lymph nodes are also a symptom, as is sudden weight loss that's not explainable by other factors. A doctor will first do a physical exam to check the lymph nodes. That will be followed by blood tests and, in some cases, imaging tests like X-rays. A sample of the lymph will also be taken, or sometimes a node will actually be removed so that it can be analyzed. (This may sound intimidating, but it's actually a fairly minor procedure.) Doctors may also use a needle to take a sample of the bone marrow itself.

An oil painting of Sir Thomas Hodgkin by the artist John Burton.

Once a lymphoma diagnosis is reached, a doctor will begin the process of staging, which is the term for figuring out how far the cancer has progressed, or what "stage" it is at. (See sidebar on page 28 for more on this.) The earlier the stage, the better the patient's outcome is likely to be. As with leukemia, stem cell transplants are an option for some people with lymphoma.

Hodgkin lymphoma has a very good survival rate, with more than 80 percent of people surviving five years or more, depending on the stage. For instance,

WHAT IS STAGING?

One thing doctors noticed about Hodgkin lymphoma was the way it moved predictably from one lymph node to the next. This march across the body inspired the notion of staging, which was developed for lymphoma patients in the 1960s. These are the basic stages of lymphoma:

- **stage I:** the malignant cells are only located in one lymph node.
- **stage II:** the malignant cells are in two lymph nodes *or* in one lymph node and one other organ, but the two sites are near each other in the body.
- **stage III:** malignant cells are found in two different areas of the body.
- **stage IV:** malignant cells are in multiple areas of the body and in other organs (for example, the lungs or the bones).

The staging system was first invented for lymphoma, but today all cancer patients are "staged" in some way. The stage of cancer has a big impact on what types of treatment the person gets. For instance, because stage I cancers are very **localized**, they are more likely to be treated with surgery, whereas later-stage cancers often require a more systemic approach, such as chemotherapy.

Although every case of cancer is unique, it is pretty safe to say that the earlier the stage a person is, the better the outcome is likely to be. This is why doctors always put such a big emphasis on screenings and early detection.

people with stage I Hodgkin have a greater than 90 percent survival rate; stage IV is more difficult, but even in those cases, the survival rate is around 65 percent.

Childhood Sarcomas

So far in this chapter, we've looked at cancers that occur when cells grow out of control in bone marrow, where blood cells are made. Sarcomas are another type of cancer that can affect the bones, muscles, and connective tissue, such as cartilage. There are a great many types of sarcomas—we will focus on the ones that occur in young people.

When people talk about "bone cancer," they usually mean osteosarcoma, which is the most common type of cancer that can develop in bones. According to the American Cancer Society, there are about 800 cases of osteosarcoma diagnosed in this country every year; about half of those are in young people.

The cellular framework that makes bones solid is called the *bone matrix*, and it has a few types of cells. *Osteoblasts* are the cells that actually make up the bone matrix, while *osteoclasts* control the growth and shape of the bone itself. Another important function of these cells is to regulate the amount of minerals that circulate in the bloodstream. Mutations in these cells are what cause osteosarcoma, in which the bone matrix grows out of control. The most common spots for this to occur are around the knees and the shoulders, but it can occur in any bone.

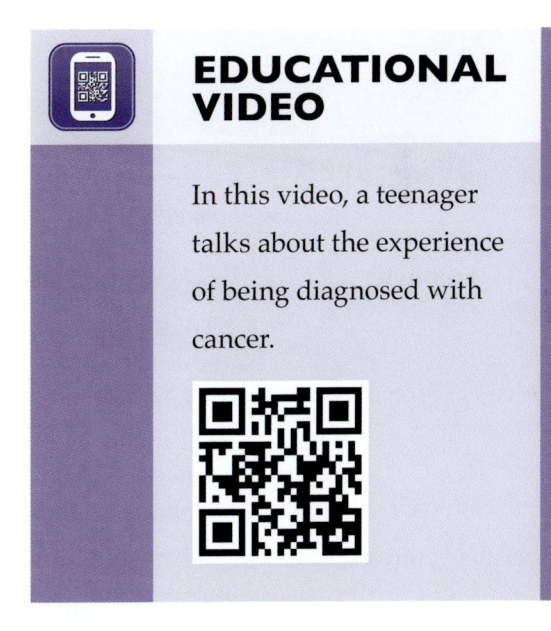

EDUCATIONAL VIDEO

In this video, a teenager talks about the experience of being diagnosed with cancer.

CANCER AND SICKLE CELL DISEASE

OSTEOSARCOMA

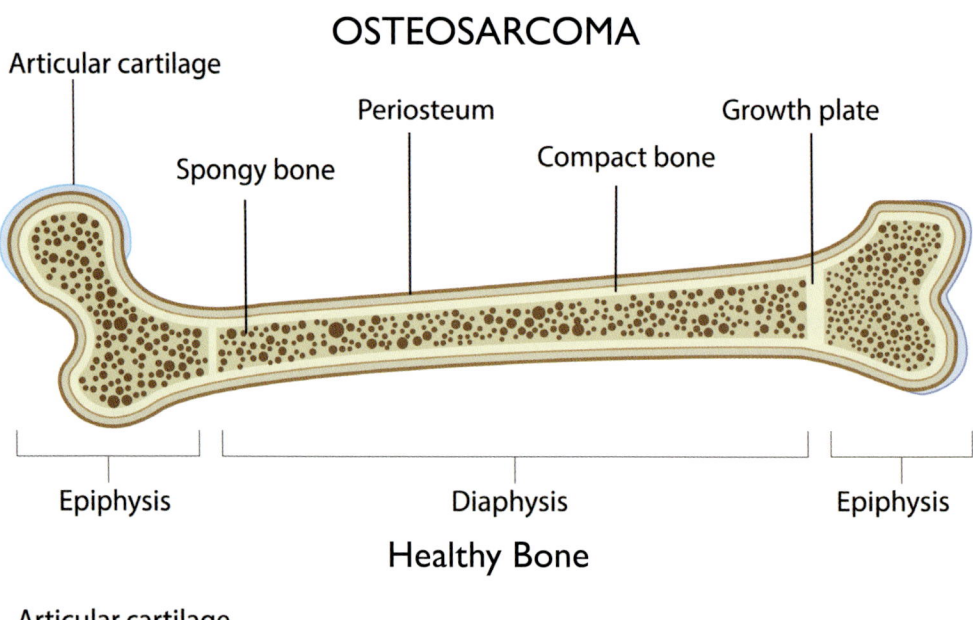

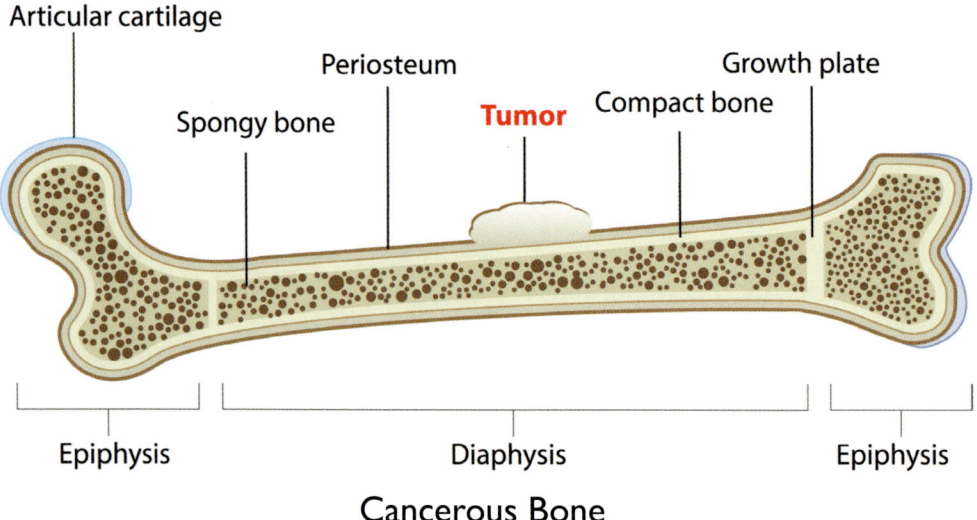

Healthy Bone

Cancerous Bone

A comparison of two bones, one healthy and one with cancer.

Osteosarcomas tend to be more common in kids than adults, probably because young people's bones are growing more quickly. Osteosarcomas are also somewhat more likely to happen in males than females. Interestingly, when they do happen to girls, they tend to happen at a younger age than in boys. Doctors theorize that this is because girls have their "growth spurt" earlier than boys do.

There are several other, more rare types of sarcomas that are also found in young people. One is called rhabdomyosarcoma, and it affects the muscle tissue. Only about 350 young people are diagnosed with this type every year.

Another type is called Ewing sarcoma, which is named for Dr. James Ewing, who first identified the tumor in 1921. Ewing sarcoma can develop in the tissue that surrounds the bones or in the bone itself. Only about 200 Americans develop Ewing sarcoma every year—about half of those are under the age of 20.

Unlike adult cancers, some of which have a connection to lifestyle choices, there is nothing anyone can do to cause or avoid childhood sarcomas. A few specific types may be inherited, and young people who had some other type of cancer that was treated with radiation may have a somewhat elevated chance of also developing bone cancer later on. But, ultimately, these conditions are not caused by anything the person did or didn't do.

Text-Dependent Questions

1. What is anemia?
2. What is staging, and why is it important?
3. What are the names of the cells that make up the bone matrix?

Research Project

Find out more about one of the types of childhood cancer discussed in this chapter. Research the specific types of treatments used for that type of cancer, and write a brief report about them.

WORDS TO UNDERSTAND

ameliorate: to make better.
biopsy: a tissue sample that's examined for diagnosis.
communicable: transferable from one person to another.
intravenously: through the veins.
ionizing radiation: a type of radiation that carries an electrical charge; X-rays are one type.
oncology: the study of cancer.

CHAPTER THREE

Living with Cancer

Diagnosing cancer in young people can be tough sometimes, because many of the symptoms look a lot like other childhood diseases. But once a cancer diagnosis is made and staged, decisions will need to be made about a treatment plan. This is not something your pediatrician will do. Instead, you'll see an oncologist, a doctor who specializes in cancer. Frequently, treatment takes place at a medical center that specializes in kids' cancer, otherwise known as pediatric **oncology**, where an entire team of doctors and nurses will collaborate on the treatment.

There's no "one-size-fits-all" treatment for cancer. In fact, there are many different options, each with its own pros and cons. A variety of factors are considered, including the part of the body affected, the person's family history, and how far the cancer has spread. This is particularly true when it comes to young people. When a young person has cancer, a lot of thought goes into not only how to treat the cancer, but also how to do so in a way that will have the smallest possible impact on the person's future.

CANCER AND SICKLE CELL DISEASE

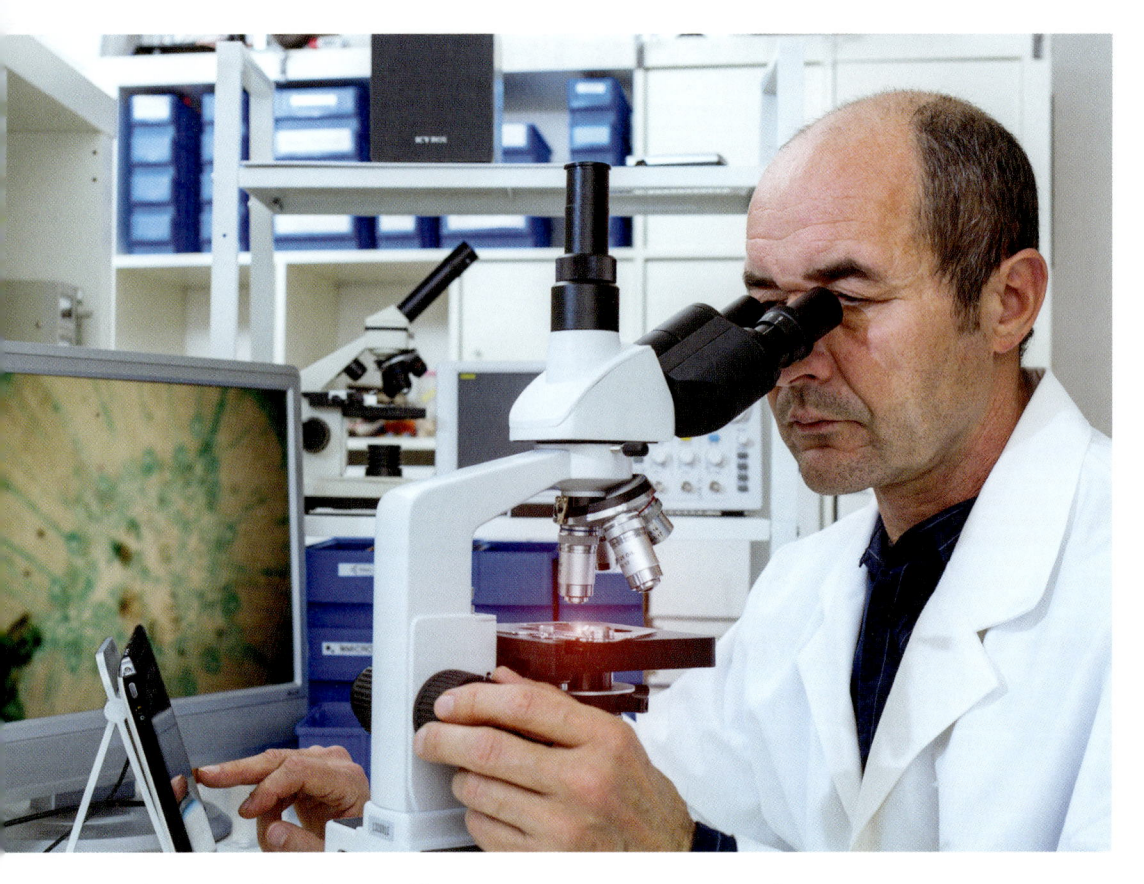

Cancer is often diagnosed by examining a tissue sample under a microscope.

Treatment Basics

This section will provide you with an overview of the basic types of treatment available. It's important to understand that every treatment plan needs to be tailored to the specific needs of the individual patient.

Surgery. Surgery is not only a common part of cancer treatment, but it also plays a role in diagnosis. That's because doctors often need to take a **biopsy** of the cancer tissue in order to figure out precisely what kinds of cells are reproducing too quickly. Surgery can also be used to remove tumors or to repair

LIVING WITH CANCER

damaged tissue. For instance, someone with osteosarcoma might undergo surgery to remove a section of bone and (often) replace it with a metal rod.

Sometimes people get preventive surgery. If a person's family history suggests that he or she is likely to develop a particular type of cancer, a decision may be made to remove a particular organ before the cancer has a chance to grow at all. Other surgeries can make it easier for people to get treated. For instance, occasionally a tube is surgically implanted in a person's body, which reduces the number of times he or she needs to get stuck with a needle. Finally, some people have reconstructive surgery after their cancer has been treated, to restore their appearance.

Radiation. There are a lot of ironies in the cancer world, and one big irony is that radiation—which is energy that travels in the form of electromagnetic

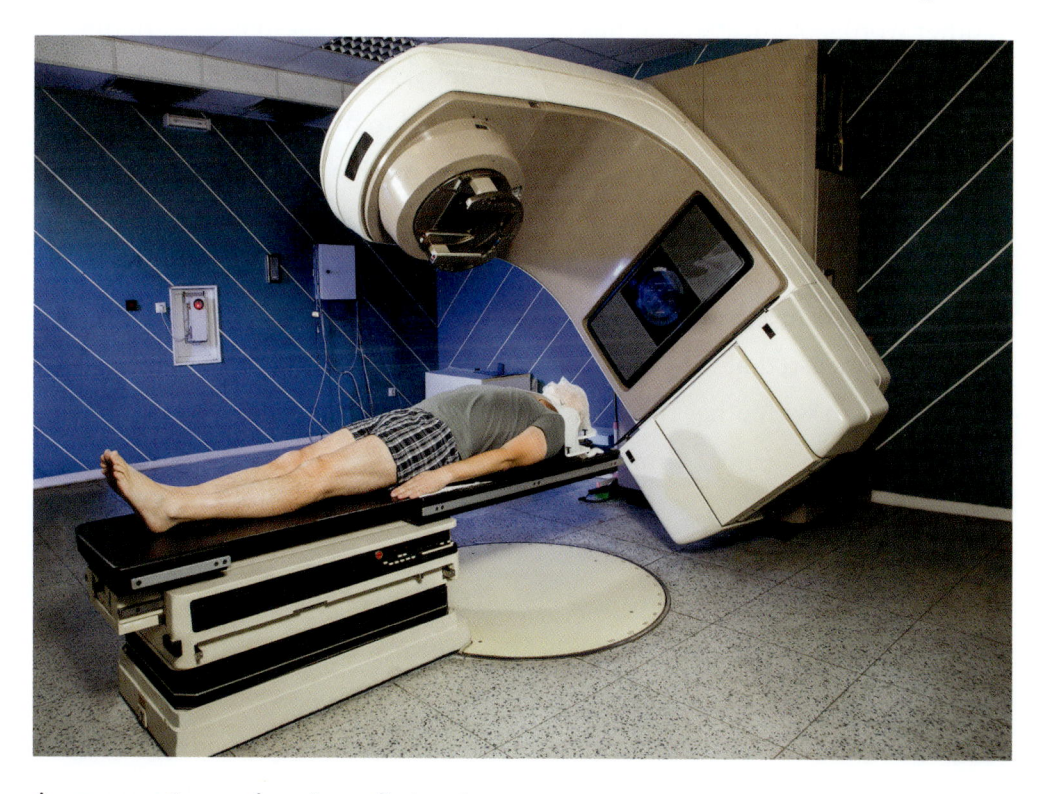

A cancer patient undergoing radiation therapy.

waves—can be both a cause of and a cure for cancer. There are many types of radiation; some are part of nature, while others are created by humans. Light from the sun is a natural type of radiation, while radio signals and microwaves are man-made types. The type of radiation used to fight cancer is called **ionizing radiation**.

Ionizing radiation affects which cells are reproducing, when they reproduce, and how quickly they reproduce. When targeted correctly, it can be used to interrupt the life cycle of cancer cells. Unfortunately, it can also kill healthy cells, which leads to some unpleasant side effects. Radiation treatment is therefore a constant balancing act between killing the "bad" cells and sparing as many "good" ones as possible.

Chemotherapy. Chemotherapy simply means "treatment with chemicals"—in other words, medications. It has some of the same trade-offs as radiation. Cancer drugs can kill cells throughout the body, which makes chemotherapy a good choice when someone's cancer has spread to more than one part of the body. But it's also very hard on the body (more on this in the next section).

Chemotherapy can be administered **intravenously**, or it can be taken orally. It's given for very limited periods, called *cycles*; someone might have a two-week cycle of chemotherapy, for example, and then not do any for a while, so that the body can recover. Chemotherapy is often used in combination with other treatments. So a person might undergo some chemotherapy to shrink a tumor, and then have surgery or radiation to remove the rest of it.

A newer type of chemotherapy is called *targeted therapy*, which involves cancer drugs that only affect cancer cells. This probably sounds like an obvious thing to do—kill the bad cells, not the good—but it took a tremendous amount of medical research to figure out precisely *how* to get a drug to attack one cell and not another. Targeted chemotherapy drugs focus on the genetic changes that cause certain cells to be cancerous. When those cells are identified, the drugs can do a couple of different things. Some can

LIVING WITH CANCER

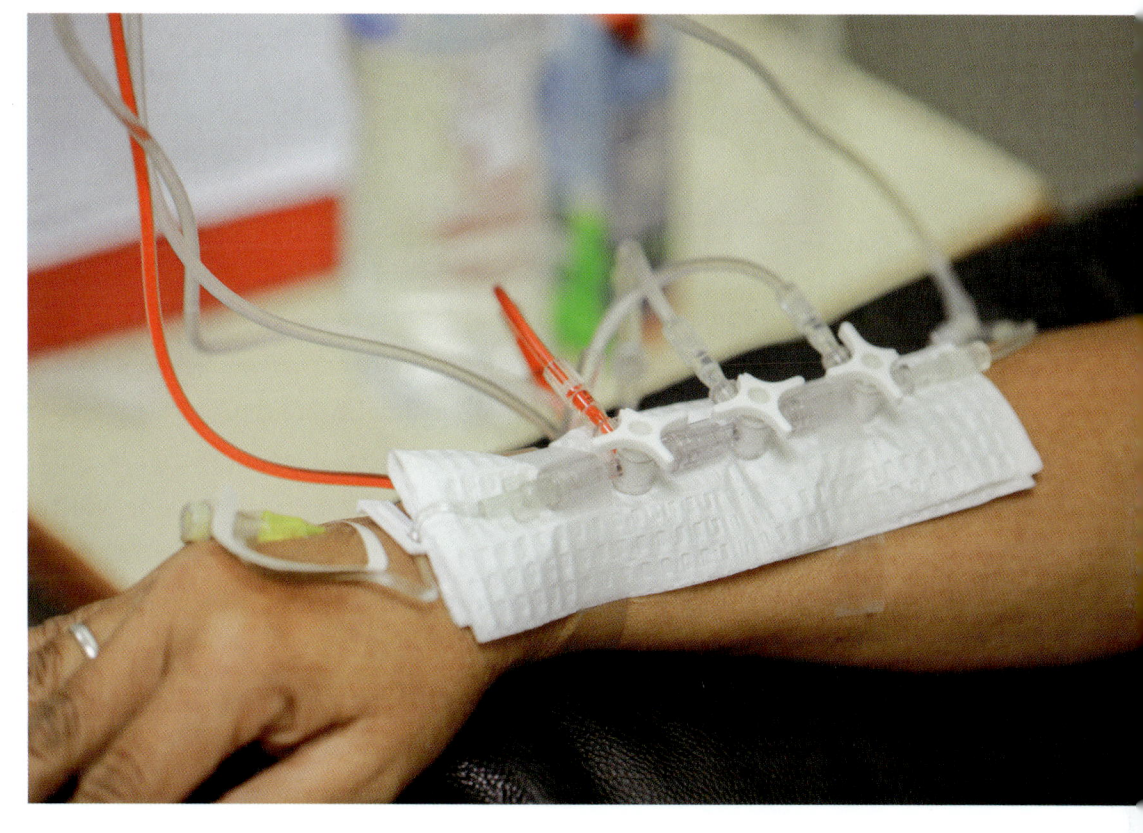

Chemotherapy is often given intravenously, but not always; it can also be given in oral form.

turn off chemical signals that cause reproduction, while others deliver what is essentially a poison directly into the cancer cells. Another method involves stopping the body from making blood vessels that support the cancer cells—essentially starving the cancer cells to death.

Another new frontier in cancer therapy is called *immunotherapy*. Since cancer is essentially a failure of the immune system to kill off malignant cells, immunotherapy works to essentially teach the body to better recognize cancer cells, and to boost the body's cancer-fighting abilities.

Researchers are also working on *cancer vaccines*, which would help the body stop cancer before it begins. The most important cancer vaccine currently on the market gives protection against the human papillomavirus (HPV), which is associated with cervical and vaginal cancer in women, penile cancer in men, and mouth and thorax cancer in both genders.

Side Effects

Cancer treatments—the exact things that are going to make you well—can actually make you feel pretty bad when you are experiencing them. Fortunately, there's a lot that doctors can do to **ameliorate** these side effects. Chemotherapy tends to cause intense nausea, for example, but there are good anti-nausea drugs that can help control this. Still, coping with the side effects of treatment can be hard.

The goal of cancer treatment is to destroy all the mutating cells. But the treatments don't just kill cancer cells—they often kill other cells as well. For example, most chemotherapy seeks out cells that divide quickly; that means cancer cells, but it also means other fast-growing cells, like hair follicles. That's why people often lose their hair during chemo. Another spot where cells grow quickly is inside the mouth and throat, so those spots are vulnerable to side effects, too, including dry mouth, sores, and a loss of taste.

Just as treatments vary from person to person, so do the side effects—some people have a lot, some very few. Problems with the digestive system are common, including nausea and vomiting, diarrhea, and an overall loss of appetite. It's also completely normal to feel incredibly tired while undergoing treatment. People who've been through it describe an overwhelming sort of fatigue, as though they could not get enough sleep to feel better. And because their immune systems are compromised, people undergoing cancer treatment are also at an increased risk for infections.

The next section has some tips that might help you cope with the side effects of treatment. But there are two important things you can do. First, talk

TO SHAVE OR NOT TO SHAVE

For many people, one of the most unpleasant side effects of cancer treatment is losing their hair. This is especially true for girls, because while it's socially acceptable for men to be bald, the same isn't really true for women. Both boys and girls may worry about feeling ugly, being stared at, and looking like "a sick person."

But remember that hair does grow back. A number of kids who've been through cancer recommend simply shaving it off—they report that it felt good to take charge of the situation, rather than waiting for their hair to fall out a little at a time. One young patient at the UCLA Daltrey/Townshend Teen Cancer Program advises her fellow patients to shave their hair while it's still healthy and "donate it to people who need it." Another said, "I was really scared about shaving my hair . . . but when I shaved my head, I've never been so happy. It's the weirdest sensation."

about your side effects with your doctor and the rest of support system—don't decide there's nothing you can do. Second, remind yourself that the side effects, as unpleasant as they are, are temporary. Try to think of them as evidence that your treatment is doing its job.

CANCER AND SICKLE CELL DISEASE

Practical Advice for Conquering Side Effects

If you are suffering from side effects of cancer treatment, here are some things to keep in mind:

- *Balance rest and activity.* It's certainly important to make sure you get enough rest. You can even let yourself take a nap during the day. At the same time, if you sleep too much during the day, you may have

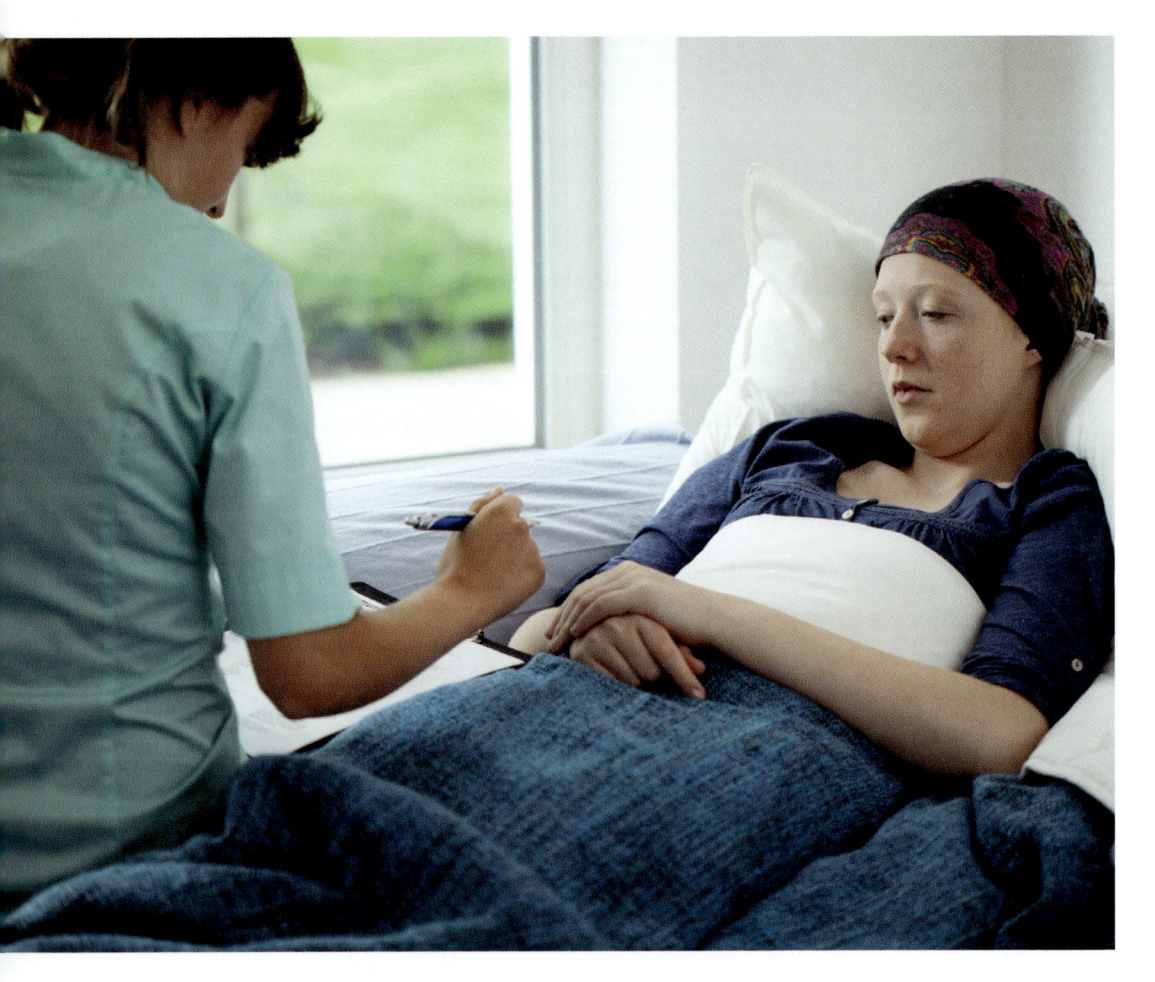

Undergoing cancer treatment can be exhausting. It's important to allow yourself lots of time to rest.

trouble getting rest at night, which ultimately can leave you feeling worse. It's important to match your resting time with periods of moving around. It may be counterintuitive when you feel so tired, but a little light exercise will actually give you more energy, not less.

EDUCATIONAL VIDEO

In this video, teens with sarcoma talk about what life is like during treatment.

- *Eat healthy food and drink lots of water.* It can be hard to even think about food if chemotherapy is making you nauseous. But giving your body fuel is really important to keep you strong and ready for the challenges ahead. Try having five or six smaller meals rather than a couple of big ones, and make sure you stay hydrated. If you're vomiting or having diarrhea, if you're constipated, or if you feel like you can't eat at all because of your upset stomach, it's really important to talk to your doctor.
- *Seek out foods that taste good to you.* Because cancer treatments can affect the cells inside your mouth, you may find that foods you used to love now taste weird or have no flavor at all. If so, it's time to experiment. If your food suddenly seems bland, try adding some spice; if it seems too bitter, try sweeter foods. You can also try using plastic utensils, which might help reduce a metallic taste.
- *Take care of your skin.* Both radiation and chemotherapy can make your skin very dry and itchy. Check with your doctor about what kinds of skin-care products are good for you. Make sure to wear loose clothing

- that doesn't chafe the affected areas, and always use sunscreen when you're outdoors.
- *Take care of your overall health.* Cancer treatment can be hard on the immune system. Remember that the treatment often targets fast-growing cells, and that includes the white blood cells that are supposed to fight off viruses and bacteria. Be sure to keep your hands washed and your treatment areas clean. As much as you can, avoid being around anyone who is sick with a cold or other **communicable** illness.

Dealing with Feelings

Physical side effects are no fun, but they are temporary, and many of them can be reduced with help from your doctor. The emotional fallout from having cancer may be the biggest challenge of all.

Although most types of cancer are more survivable than ever before, it would be wrong to pretend that cancer is not serious or, oftentimes, terrifying. This is especially true for young people, who tend to feel invulnerable and aren't prepared to come face-to-face with their own mortality. You may feel very angry at times, and that the situation you're in is not fair. And you're right, it's not fair. It's perfectly okay to be angry, sad, depressed, or scared. All those feelings are valid. Here are some suggestions that may help you get through the bad times:

- *Get informed.* Sometimes when we feel scared, it can be tempting to stick our heads in the proverbial sand and just not want to know. But a lack of knowledge about your condition is likely to make you more anxious in the long run. The solution is to learn as much as you can. Talk to your doctor about where to find reliable, comprehensible sources of information about your specific condition and treatments.

LIVING WITH CANCER

- *Try to connect.* When you're feeling upset and overwhelmed, it can be helpful to talk with other people who have been where you are. Again, your treatment team is the best source of information about support groups in your area. You can also look online. The nonprofit group CancerCare offers a wide variety of online, telephone, and in-person support (go to www.cancercare.org).
- *Make time for non-cancer stuff.* Sometimes it may feel like cancer is taking over your whole life. You may not be going to school as often, which can make it easy to lose contact with your friends and your pre-cancer life. Try to save some time and energy for doing things you enjoyed before you got sick.

It's important to maintain friendships even when you're sick; friends will help sustain you as you face the challenges ahead.

WHEN A FRIEND HAS CANCER

When somebody you care about is seriously ill, it can be hard to know what to say or how to act. Here are some suggestions:

- Do some research on your own to find out about your friend's condition. Having a basic understanding of the type of cancer your friend has will make the whole situation less mysterious.
- Be ready to talk—or not talk. Some people who have cancer like to talk about their illness, their treatment, and all the various side effects. It's okay to talk about that stuff, and it's okay to ask questions. But some people really don't want to talk about it, and that's okay, too. Follow your friend's lead with regard to how much he or she wants to talk about the particulars.
- Make yourself available. Cancer treatment can be all-consuming at times, and your friend may not be able to hang out as much as before. Keep inviting your friend to do things anyway, even if he or she is busy or simply tired. Let him or her know that you're around and that you'll still be around when the treatment is over. Even just a quick text to say hi can mean the world to somebody who is in treatment.
- Remember that your friend is still the same person. If your buddy used to like video games, or basketball, or musicals, he or she still likes all that stuff. Cancer has not made your friend into someone else.

LIVING WITH CANCER

- *Be kind to yourself.* You may have some bad days, and that's okay. Treat yourself as well as you would treat a loved one who's sick. And remember, most young people who get cancer also get past it. This is one period in your life—it is a very difficult period, but it's a period that will end. You are not your illness, you are a person *with* an illness.

Text-Dependent Questions

1. What are the main types of cancer treatment?
2. What are the challenges of undergoing chemotherapy?
3. What are some things friends can do to help someone with cancer?

Research Project

Research what kinds of accommodations your school makes for students fighting cancer. What are the attendance policies? What about homework? Is counseling available through the school? Create a pamphlet that could explain what you've learned to someone who needs it.

WORDS TO UNDERSTAND

dominant: in genetics, a dominant trait is expressed in a child even when the trait is only inherited from one parent.
hemoglobin: a component in red blood cells that carries oxygen.
jaundice: a condition that can be caused by the breakdown of blood cells, causing the skin and the whites of the eyes to develop a yellowish color.
malaria: a mosquito-borne blood disease common in very warm locales.
recessive: in genetics, a recessive trait will only be expressed if a child inherits it from both parents.
vasoconstrictor: something that causes blood vessels to tighten.

CHAPTER FOUR

Living with Sickle Cell Disease

Cancer is ultimately a problem with cell growth: too many of the wrong cells grow too quickly for the body to dispose of them. The blood disorder called sickle cell disease is similar to cancer in the sense that it, too, involves out-of-control cell growth. But sickle cell is not the same as cancer. People don't mysteriously develop it at various points in life. It is a genetic condition, meaning that people are born with it, and it causes chronic health problems throughout life. As many as 100,000 Americans are living with sickle cell disease, making it the country's most common genetic disorder.

Blood Cells

Healthy red blood cells are round—under a microscope they may look like donuts or discs. These cells contain **hemoglobin** A (HbA), and HbA's job is to transport oxygen from the lungs to the rest of the body. But the red blood cells of someone with sickle cell don't have HbA; instead, they have hemoglobin S (HbS) or

CANCER AND SICKLE CELL DISEASE

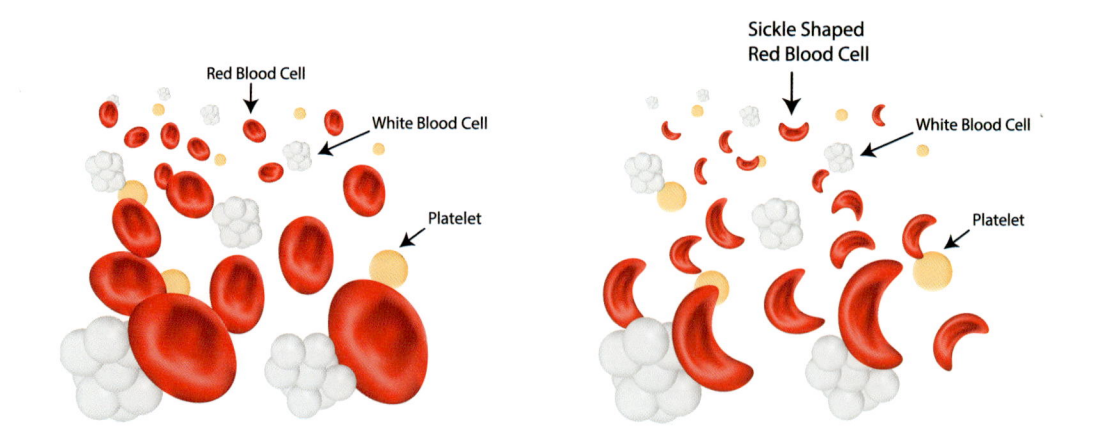

This diagram shows the difference in shape between healthy blood cells and sickle cells.

hemoglobin C (HbC). The presence of abnormal hemoglobin causes the red blood cells to be stickier and oddly shaped. In fact, the name "sickle cell" comes from the crescent-shaped farm implement called a sickle, which the cells resemble.

Sickle cell disease results in a variety of problems. Sickle cells do not live as long as regular blood cells do—healthy blood cells live around three months, while sickle cells may only live three weeks. This means it's very hard for the body to keep up with the production of new cells. Consequently, people with sickle cell disease often have anemia, because their bodies can't make the healthy red blood cells they need. Anemia results in fatigue, rapid heartbeat, shortness of breath, and dizziness, among other symptoms.

In addition, the shape of sickle cells can cause them to clump up more easily, which blocks blood flow. This can cause pain, which is sometimes referred to as a pain crisis or pain episode. This episode which can last anywhere from a few minutes to a number of weeks. Pain episodes can range from mild, for which you need only over-the-counter pain medications like aspirin, to severe, which requires hospitalization. Some people with the sickle cell have to deal with crises on a regular basis, while others are luckier and only have a pain crisis once or twice a year.

LIVING WITH SICKLE CELL DISEASE

SYMPTOMS OF ANEMIA

Respiratory — Shortness of breath

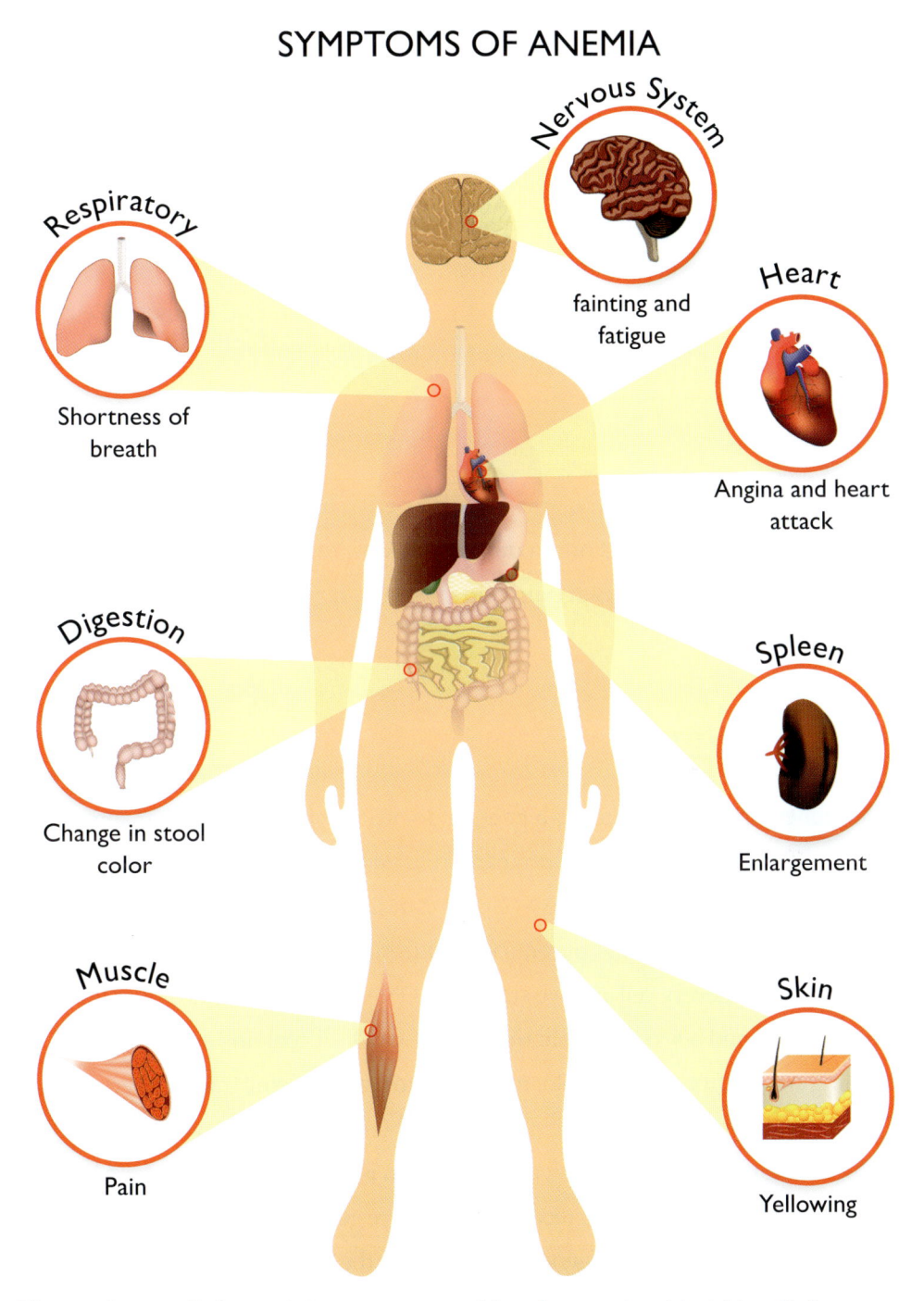

Nervous System — fainting and fatigue

Heart — Angina and heart attack

Digestion — Change in stool color

Spleen — Enlargement

Muscle — Pain

Skin — Yellowing

The condition called anemia is a common problem for people with sickle cell disease.

CANCER AND SICKLE CELL DISEASE

SYMPTOMS OF SICKLE CELL DISEASE

- anemia
- **jaundice**
- swollen hands and feet
- intense pain, especially in chest, bones, and joints
- pneumonia (especially in babies)
- eye problems

A whole range of other problems can also occur, from pneumonia to strokes, infections, eye problems, and organ damage. A very serious condition called *acute chest syndrome* causes chest pain and severe difficulty breathing when the clumps happen in the lungs.

Who Gets Sickle Cell?

As mentioned above, sickle cell is a genetic disorder, which means that someone inherits it from their parents. But not everyone who has the gene for sickle cell disease actually develops the illness. Understanding this requires a quick review of how genes are passed from parents to children.

At the center of every cell are two strands of DNA; one strand comes from the person's mother, and one comes from the father. Our DNA contains instructions for everything we are, from our eye color to our risk for cancer. Some traits are **recessive,** and some are **dominant**—the classic example teachers love to use is eye color, in which the colors blue and green are recessive, while brown is dominant. In order for a baby to have blue eyes, he or she needs to receive the blue-eye gene from both Mom and Dad. If the baby receives the blue-eye gene from Mom but the brown-eye gene from Dad, the baby will have brown eyes, because brown is a dominant trait.

LIVING WITH SICKLE CELL DISEASE

The sickle cell trait (SCT) works the same way. SCT is a recessive trait, so a baby would need to receive it from both Mom and Dad in order to develop the condition. Here's the tricky part, though: since SCT is recessive, a person can have one copy of the gene and not know it. That means it's easy for two otherwise healthy people to have a child who ends up with sickle cell disease.

There are two bits of good news, though. First, it is not definite that a child of two parents with SCT will have the problem. It only happens about 25 percent of the time. Second, there are now screening tests available that can help would-be parents be aware of the potential problem before it happens. In the United States, all newborns have been screened for SCT since 2006. (If you don't know your status but want to, your pediatrician should have the information in your record; if not, a simple blood test can determine it.)

Sickle cell disease is most often passed down in African American families, but that is not always the case; other ethnicities can carry the trait as well.

CANCER AND SICKLE CELL DISEASE

One very common myth about sickle cell disease is that it's a condition that's only of concern to African Americans. It is true that the majority of people with sickle cell are African American, but estimates put the number somewhere between 60 and 80 percent. That means that there are many thousands of people with the disorder who are of other races. The SCT can also be carried by people of Hispanic, Middle Eastern, Indian, and Mediterranean descent.

WHAT'S MALARIA GOT TO DO WITH IT?

If left untreated, sickle cell disease is likely to shorten the life span of people who have it. Today, people do not have to worry as much about this, but before treatments were available, people with sickle cell tended to not live as long as healthy people. This left researchers confused. The scientist Linus Pauling figured out in 1949 that sickle cell is inherited from parents. But if most people with the disease did not used to live long enough to become parents, why did the mutation continue to occur? Wouldn't logic suggest that a life-shortening gene mutation would become increasingly rare and finally die out entirely?

It turns out that the trait is not entirely bad. The mutation originated in places where another deadly disease, malaria, is common. Like sickle cell, malaria is a blood disease. But malaria is caused by parasites, which infect humans via mosquito bites. It turns out that the sickle cell mutation protects people from malaria. Exactly how this occurred was a mystery for a long time, but in 2011 scientists discovered that the sickle cells actually prevent the malaria parasite from harming the host. They theorized that the sickle cell trait continues to be passed on because it is actually helpful to people who live in places where malaria is common.

LIVING WITH SICKLE CELL DISEASE

Parents

Father — carrier

Mother — carrier

Child — healthy

Child — carrier

Child — carrier

Child — has sickle cell disease

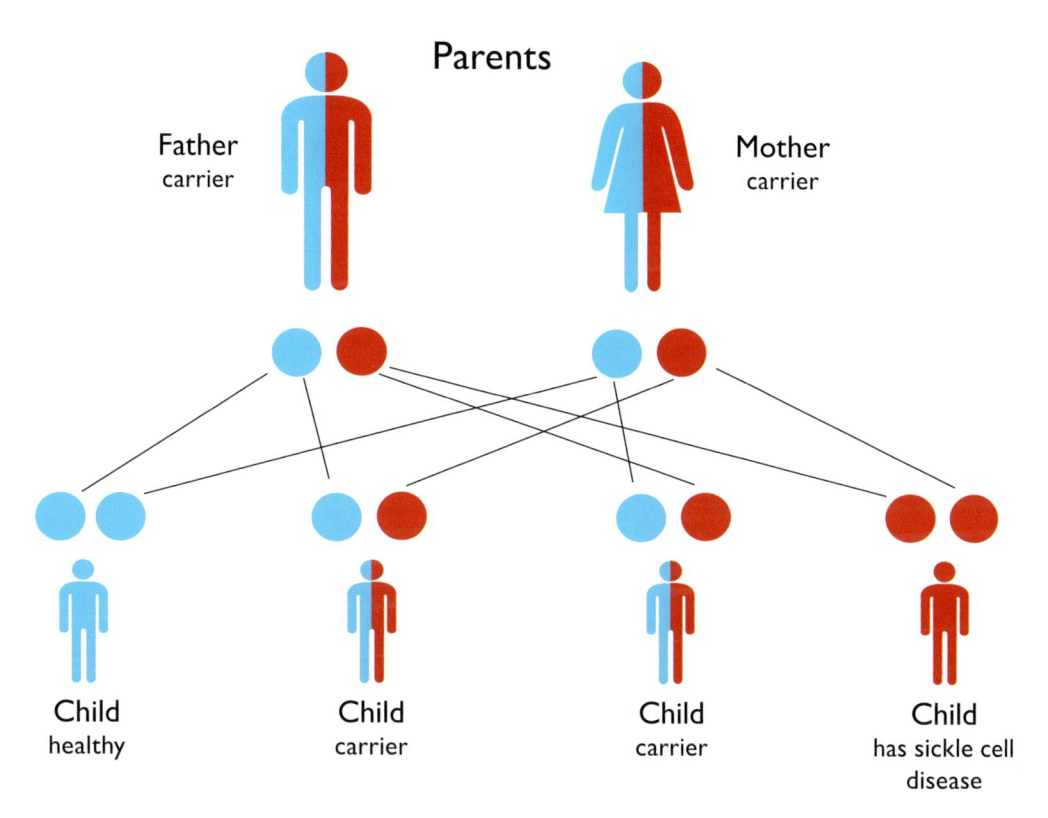

This diagram shows how two parents who both carry the recessive sickle cell trait might pass it along to their children.

Evolving Understanding

Like so much of our scientific knowledge, our understanding of sickle cell didn't appear in a single, forehead-slapping, "eureka!" moment. It took many years of study and the contributions of many scientists to get us where we are today.

A doctor named James Herrick published the first description of sickle cell in 1910; the patient was a man from the Caribbean, and Herrick noticed the strange shape of his blood cells. The following year, the details of a second case were published. This time it was a woman. At first she was thought to have anemia, except her symptoms were too strange to be simply that.

CANCER AND SICKLE CELL DISEASE

Although Herrick had used the term "sickle-shaped" to describe the blood cells, the name *sickle cell anemia* was coined in 1922 by Verne Mason, who was also the person to notice that the people with this condition all hailed from the same general part of the world.

Discoveries continued to mount, and in 1933 Dr. Lemuel Diggs drew a distinction between "active" sickle cell disease (meaning people who were ill) and "latent" sickle cell disease (meaning people who carried the trait but were not ill). In 1949 the scientist Linus Pauling was able to identify the role of hemoglobin in the disease, pointing out that sufferers had HbS instead of HbA.

Managing Your Sickle Cell Disease

A few decades ago, a book like this wouldn't have had a chapter about "living with sickle cell," because children with the condition often didn't live far beyond

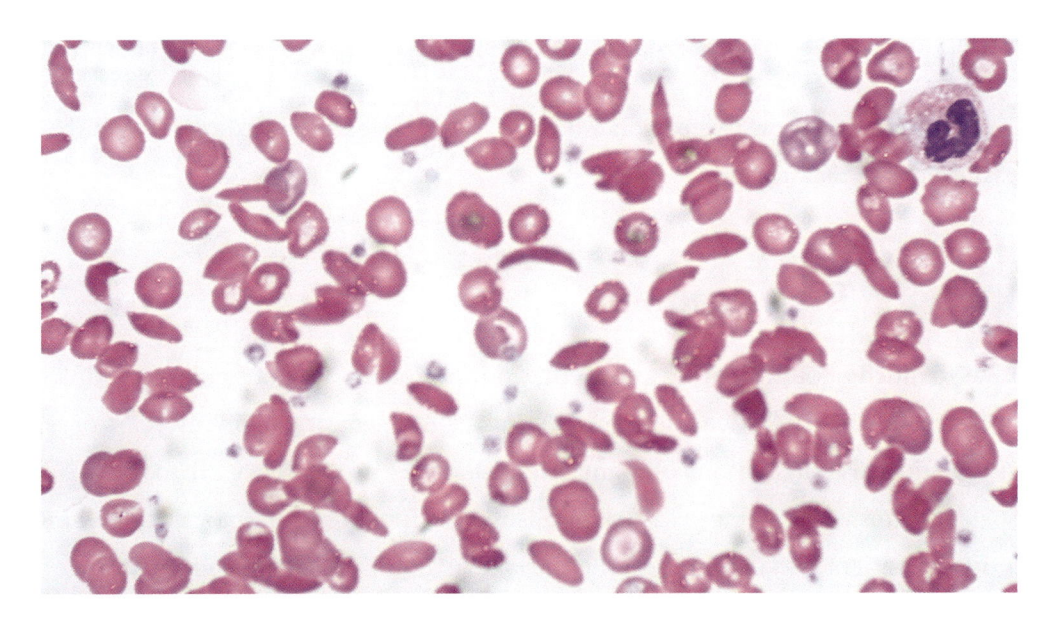

The blood cells of someone with sickle cell enlarged under a microscope. The telltale sickle shapes are easily visible.

LIVING WITH SICKLE CELL DISEASE

childhood. Adults with sickle cell were rare; nowadays, it's a chronic but manageable disease. The drop in mortality rates is great news for people born with the condition. But it has led to new challenges.

In the medical world, less attention has been focused on the needs of adults with sickle cell disease. As children with sickle cell grow into adulthood, they sometimes have difficulty finding help and support. For instance, clinics primarily designed for children may not be set up for the needs of adult patient.

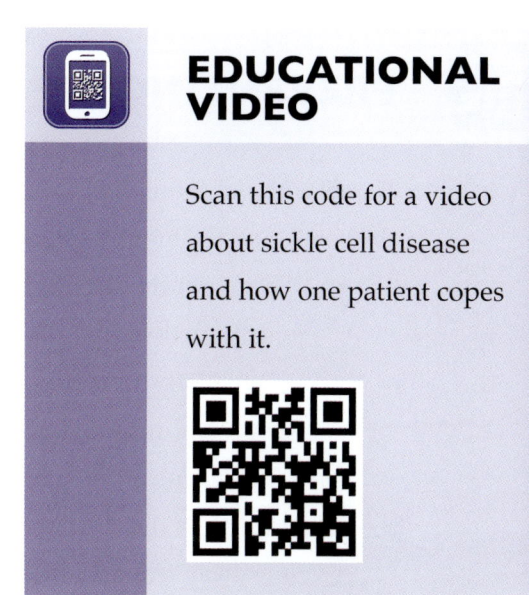

When we're kids, we all depend on our caregivers to make most of the choices and medical decisions for us. As young adults, it's increasingly important for us to take more and more responsibility for ourselves and our care.

Three initial steps will help begin this process. First, it's true what they say: knowledge is power. It's important to learn as much as possible about your condition. Second, because there is so much for people with sickle cell to remember, it's smart to keep a written record of appointments, timing of medication doses and procedures, shots taken and still needed to avoid infections, and any other health-enhancing activities.

Third, with advice from a doctor or other health professional, teens with the disorder should plan a progressive fitness and health program that includes adequate sleep, regular exercise, and nutrition support. In addition to exercise, two other factors important to health for people with the disease are managing stress and avoiding infections. (See sidebar on page 56.)

EDUCATIONAL VIDEO

Scan this code for a video about sickle cell disease and how one patient copes with it.

CANCER AND SICKLE CELL DISEASE

PREVENTING INFECTION

People with sickle cell are prone to infections, especially in the blood, the bones, and the lungs. Here are some tips about how to keep healthy:

- Wash your hands frequently with soap and water, and take your time doing it—20 seconds at least. Also, be sure to wash up when preparing food or eating.
- Keep your immunizations up to date, and make sure you get a flu vaccine annually.
- Drink a lot of water and follow a healthy, varied diet.
- Stay away from alcohol and caffeine. Alcohol causes fluid loss, which can make sickle-cell pain worse, and caffeine is a **vasoconstrictor**, meaning that it causes blood vessels to shrink, which, again, can worsen pain.
- Do not smoke under any circumstances. Tobacco smoke is bad for everyone, but people with sickle cell disease need to take this admonition especially seriously. Tobacco use reduces the amount of oxygen taken in by the lungs.

Text-Dependent Question

1. What is hemoglobin?
2. Roughly how many Americans have sickle cell disease?
3. What should people with sickle cell disease do to try to avoid infections?

Research Project

Create an informational poster or pamphlet about sickle cell disease, including how to reduce the likelihood of a pain crisis.

FURTHER READING

Bucher, Julia A., Peter S. Houts, and Terri B. Ades, eds. *American Cancer Society Complete Guide to Family Caregiving.* 2nd ed. Atlanta, GA: American Cancer Society, 2011.

Morrison, Candis, and Charles S. Hesdorffer. *John's Hopkins Patients' Guide to Leukemia.* Sudbury, MA: Jones and Bartlett, 2010.

National Cancer Institute. "Children with Cancer: A Guide for Parents." https://www.cancer.gov/publications/patient-education/guide-for-parents.

National Cancer Institute. "Side Effects." https://www.cancer.gov/about-cancer/treatment/side-effects.

Platt, Alan F., James Eckman, and Lewis Hsu. *Hope and Destiny: The Patient and Parent's Guide to Sickle Cell Disease and Sickle Cell Trait.* Revised 4th ed. Indianapolis, IN: Hilton Publishing, 2016.

Thornton, Denise. *Living with Cancer: The Ultimate Teen Guide.* Lanham, MD: Scarecrow Press, 2011.

Vescia, Monique, Alvin Silverstein, Virginia Silverstein, and Laura Silverstein Nunn. *What You Can Do about Sickle Cell Disease.* New York: Enslow Publishing, 2016.

Educational Videos

Chapter One: Cancer Research UK. "How Healthy Cells Divide." https://youtu.be/zR8rIPcOZMY.

Chapter Two: Julia Elizabeth. "My Cancer Story: Getting Diagnosed." https://youtu.be/IIjzl4E7hcI.

Chapter Three: UCLA Health. "Teen Cancer Stories." https://youtu.be/y1Lablc6NQg.

Chapter Four: American Society of Hematology. "Sickle Cell Anemia: A Patient's Journey." https://youtu.be/2CsgXHdWqVs.

SERIES GLOSSARY

accommodation: an arrangement or adjustment to a new situation; for example, schools make accommodations to help students cope with illness.

anemia: an illness caused by a lack of red blood cells.

autoimmune: type of disorder where the body's immune system attacks the body's tissues instead of germs.

benign: not harmful.

biofeedback: a technique used to teach someone how to control some bodily functions.

capillaries: tiny blood vessels that carry blood from larger blood vessels to body tissues.

carcinogens: substances that can cause cancer to develop.

cerebellum: the back part of the brain; it controls movement.

cerebrum: the front part of the brain; it controls many higher-level thinking and functions.

cholesterol: a waxy substance associated with fats that coats the inside of blood vessels, causing cardiovascular disease.

cognitive: related to conscious mental activities, such as learning and thinking.

communicable: transferable from one person to another.

congenital: a condition or disorder that exists from birth.

correlation: a connection between different things that suggests they may have something to do with one another.

dominant: in genetics, a dominant trait is expressed in a child even when the trait is only inherited from one parent.

environmental factors: anything that affects how people live, develop, or grow. Climate, diet, and pollution are examples.

genes: units of hereditary information.

hemorrhage: bleeding from a broken blood vessel.

hormones: substances the body produces to instruct cells and tissues to perform certain actions.

inflammation: redness, swelling, and tenderness in a part of the body in response to infection or injury.

SERIES GLOSSARY

insulin: a hormone produced in the pancreas that controls cells' ability to absorb glucose.

lymphatic system: part of the human immune system; transports white blood cells around the body.

malignant: harmful; relating to tumors, likely to spread.

mutation: a change in the structure of a gene; some mutations are harmless, but others may cause disease.

neurological: relating to the nervous system (including the brain and spinal cord).

neurons: specialized cells found in the central nervous system (the brain and spinal cord).

occupational therapy: a type of therapy that teaches one how to accomplish tasks and activities in daily life.

oncology: the study of cancer.

orthopedic: dealing with deformities in bones or muscles.

prevalence: how common or uncommon a disease is in any given population.

prognosis: the forecast for the course of a disease that predicts whether a person with the disease will get sicker, recover, or stay the same.

progressive disease: a disease that generally gets worse as time goes on.

psychomotor: relating to movement or muscle activity resulting from mental activity.

recessive: in genetics, a recessive trait will only be expressed if a child inherits it from both parents.

remission: an improvement in or disappearance of someone's symptoms of disease; unlike a cure, remission is usually temporary.

resilience: the ability to bounce back from difficult situations.

seizure: an event caused by unusual brain activity resulting in physical or behavior changes.

syndrome: a condition with a set of associated symptoms.

ulcers: a break or sore in skin or tissue where cells disintegrate and die. Infections may occur at the site of an ulcer.

INDEX

Illlustrations are indicated by page numbers in *italic* type.

A

active disease, 54
acute chest syndrome, 50
acute myeloid leukemia (AML), 23–24
adults, 17, 30, 55
African Americans, 51–52
alcohol, 56
ALL (childhood acute lymphoblastic leukemia), 23–24
American Cancer Society, 23, 29
Americans, 31, 47, 51–52, 56
anemia, 20, 25, 48, *49*
anger, 42
antibiotics, 25
anti-nausea drugs, 38
antioxidants, 19
asbestos, 14

B

benign, 8, 18
biopsy, 32, 34
bladder, 17, 18
blame, 19
bleeding, 25–26
blood cells, 9, 18, 47–48, 50, *54*
bone cancer, 29, 31
bone marrow, 10, 18, 21–24, 26, 27, 29
bone matrix, 29
bones, 17, 21–22, 29, *30*, 31
breast cancer, 13, 15
breath shortness, 48
bronchitis, 25
bruising, 25

C

caffeine, 56
calcium, 21
cancer, 8–19
  background, 9
  blame, 19
  causes, 13–15, 31
  cell division, 9–12
  mutants, 15
  smoking and, 17, 18
  types, 15–18
  see also living with cancer
Cancer Care, 43
cancer-causing agents, 14
carcinogens, 8, 14, 19
carcinomas, 17
cartilage, 17, 29
cell reproduction (mitosis), 10–11, 13, 36–37
cells, 38, *48*
central nervous system (CNS) tumors, 18
cervical cancer, 38
chemotherapy, 25, 26, 28, 36–38
childhood acute lymphoblastic leukemia (ALL), 23–24
childhood sarcomas, 29, 30–31
choices, 19
chronic illnesses, 25, 55
cigarettes, 14, 17
clothing suggestions, 42–43
colds, 25, 42
colon cancer, 14, 18
communicable illness, 32, 42
compact bone, 21
connective tissue, 17, 29

INDEX

coping, 38, 39
crises, 48
Crohn's disease, 25
cures, 17, 25
cycles, 36

D

Dana Farber Cancer Institute, 17
depression, 42
detection, 28
diagnosis, 19, 23, 26, 29, 31, 33, *34*
diet, 19, 41, 55, 56
digestive system, 38
Diggs, Lemuel, 54
dizziness, 48
DNA, 11, 14, 50
donors, 26
drugs, 26, 36–37, 38

E

emotions, 42
environment, 15
epilepsy, 25
epithelial cells, 8, 17
erythrocytes (red blood cells), 22
ethnicity and sickle cell disease, *51*, 52
Ewing, James, 31
Ewing sarcoma, 31
exercise, 19, 39, 41, 55
exposure, 14, 15, 17
eye problems, 50

F

family history, 14
fatigue, 25, 27, 38, 48
feelings, 42–43, 44
fever, 25, 27
flu, 27, 56
friends, 43, 44

G

genes, 8, 13, 14, 15, 47, 50–51
genetic mutations, 26, 52
growth spurt, 31

H

hair, 38–39
hand washing, 56
health care, 42, 55
hemoglobin, 46, 47–48, 54
HER2 gene, 15
hereditary cancer syndromes, 13–15
Herrick, James, 53–54
Hodgkin, Thomas, 26–27
Hodgkin lymphoma, 17, 18, 26, 28
human papillomavirus (HPV), 38

I

immune systems, 24, 25, 38
immunotherapy, 37
implants, 35
infections, 38, 50, 55–56
information sources, 42
International Agency for Research on Cancer, 14
intravenous, 32, 36
ionizing radiation, 32, 36

J

jaundice, 46, 50

K

kidneys, 26
kids and cancer, 20–31
    bones and, 21–22
    and hereditary cancer syndromes, 13
    leukemia and, 23, 24, 25–26
    lymphoma and, 26–27, 29
    sarcomas in, 29–31

staging, 28
survival rates of, 25
types of cancer in, 16–18
kindness, 45
knowledge, 42

L
latent disease, 54
lawsuits, 18
lead, 14
leukemias, 18, 23, 24, 25–26
life span, 52
lifestyle, 19, 31
liver, 26
living with cancer, 32–45, 38–39
   dealing with feelings, 41–45
   side effects, 38–42
   treatments, 34–38
localized, 20, 28
locations of cancer, *16*
lungs, 17, 18, 47, 50, 56
lymphatic system, 8, 11, *12*, 26, 27, 28
lymphocytes (white blood cells), 17, 22, 23, 26
lymphoma, 17, 18, 26–27, 28

M
malaria, 46, 52
malignant, 8, 13, 18
Mason, Verne, 54
melanomas, 17
metastasis, 12
minerals, 29
mitosis (cell reproduction), 10–11, 13, 36–37
moles, 17
monitoring, 25
moral judgments, 19
mortality, 42, 55
mouth cancer, 38

muscles, 29, 31
mutations, 8, 11, 13–15, 18, 26, 29, 52
myeloid cells, 20, 23

N
National Cancer Institute, 13
National Toxicology Program, 14
nausea, 38
non-Hodgkin lymphoma, 17, 18, 26

O
older people, 17, 18
oncogenes, 15
oncology, 32, 33
online help, 43
organ damage, 50
osteoclasts, 29
osteosarcoma, 29, 30–31, 35
oxygen, 47, 56

P
pain, 26, 48, 50, 56
parasites, 52
Pauling, Linus, 52, 54
pediatric oncology, 33
penile cancer, 38
pneumonia, 50
precancerous cells, 11
prognosis, 8, 9

R
radiation, 14, 31, 35–36
rapid heartbeat, 48
recessive traits, 46, 50, *53*
reconstructive surgery, 35
recurrence, 20, 25
red blood cells (erythrocytes), 22
red marrow, 22

INDEX

resting, 40–41
rhabdomyosarcoma, 31
risk, 14, 38, 50

S
sadness, 42
sarcomas, 17, 28, 29, 30–31
screening, 9, 28, 51
sickle cell anemia, 54
sickle cell disease, 25, 46–57
   blood cells, 47–48, 50
   malaria and, 52
   managing, 54–55
   preventing, 56
   understanding, 53–54
   who gets, 50–52
sickle cell trait (SCT), 51
side effects, 36–42, 44
skeletons, 21
skin cancers, 17
skin care, 41–42
smoking, 14, 17, 18, 56
somatic mutations, 14
sore joints, 25
spongy bone, 21
staging, 27, 28, 33
stem cells, 22, 23, 26, 27
stomach, 17, 26, 41
stress management, 55
strokes, 50
support system, 38, 39
surgery, 25, 28, 34–35
survivors, 9, 23, 25, 27, 29
symptoms
  of anemia, *49*
  leukemia, *24*, 25
  of lymphoma, 27
  sickle cell disease, 50

T
targeted therapy, 36
therapy, radiation, *35*
thorax cancer, 38
throat cancer, 18
tobacco, 14, 19, 56
toxins, 14, 17
TP53 gene, 15
transplants, 26, 27
treatments, 9, 15
  basic, 34–37
  for leukemia, 26
  for melanomas, 17
  plans for, 33
  staging for, 28
  team for, 43
tumors, 13–14, 17–18, 25, 34, 36
tumor suppressor genes, 15
type 1 diabetes, 25

U
undifferentiated cells, 20, 22

V
vaccines, 37–38, 56
vaginal cancer, 38
vasoconstrictor, 46, 56
vitamins, 19

W
weight loss, 27
white blood cells (lymphocytes), 17, 18, 22, 23–24, 26, 42

X
X-rays, 14, 15, 27

ABOUT THE ADVISOR

Heather Pelletier, Ph.D., is a pediatric staff psychologist at Rhode Island Hospital/Hasbro Children's Hospital with a joint appointment as a clinical assistant professor in the departments of Psychiatry and Human Behavior and Pediatrics at the Warren Alpert Medical School of Brown University. She is also the director of behavioral pain medicine in the division of Children's Integrative therapies, Pain management and Supportive care (CHIPS) in the department of Pediatrics at Hasbro Children's Hospital. Dr. Pelletier provides clinical services to children in various medical specialty clinics at Hasbro Children's Hospital, including the pediatric gastroenterology, nutrition, and liver disease clinics.

ABOUT THE AUTHOR

H. W. Poole is a writer and editor of books for young people, including the sets, Families Today and Mental Illnesses and Disorders (Mason Crest). She created the Horrors of History series (Charlesbridge) and the Ecosystems series (Facts On File). She has also been responsible for many critically acclaimed reference books, including *Political Handbook of the World* (CQ Press) and the *Encyclopedia of Terrorism* (SAGE).

PHOTO CREDITS

Cover: iStock/jessicaphoto
iStock: 40 KatarzynaBialasiewicz; 44 FatCamera
Shutterstock: 10 Designua; 12 Alila Medical Media; 13 Designua; 16 moj0j0; 18 Out of Time; 22 NoPainNoGain; 23 Alila Medical Media; 24 Designua; 30 joshya; 34 science photo; 35 adriaticfoto; 37 Chaikom; 39 Cleomiu; 43 Photographee.eu; 48 joshya; 49 Designua; 51 Monkey Business Images; 53 Zuzanae
Wellcome Images: 27
Wikimedia: 55 Ed Uthman

NOV -- 2019

NOV -- 2019